QUILTING CALAMITY

A QUILTING COZY MYSTERY

KATHRYN MYKEL

Dragonfly's Press

Edited by Mia Quinn, www.editor.niaquinn.com
Proofread by Nicole Zoltack
Beta Read by Nola Li Barr at Tapioca Press, Jessica Fraser, and Kirsten Moore at thebestbetareader@gmail.com
Cover Design by PixelSquirrel at www.etsy.com/shop/PixelSquirrel
Formatted by Nola Li Barr at Tapioca Press

This book is dedicated to my amazing editor, Nia Quinn

Special thanks to all of my family, friends & peers.

ALSO BY KATHRYN MYKEL

Quilting Cozy Mysteries

Sewing Suspicion

Quilting Calamity

Pressing Matters

For more fun content and new releases,

sign up for her newsletter

or join her and her thReaders

on Facebook

at Author Kathryn Mykel

or Books For Quilters.

CONTENTS

INTRODUCTION

Alex didn't know her life was about to change when she walked into Celia Moore's travel agency, Destinations. Just a few days after returning to her hometown her adoptive grandmother, Nona, was murdered. Alex couldn't have imagined that she would be indirectly responsible for her death. An unassuming manila envelope only provided slight relief from the guilt.

The envelope contained letters to Alex, Nona's son Jack, and his daughter Charlotte. Jack's and Charlotte's letters were typical *I love you and wish you a good life* letters, but the one Nona had left for Alex was different. This letter was the start of the upcoming journey and her new life as the matriarch of Spruce Street.

However, instead of assuming the role as matriarch, Alex was chasing the posthumous whims of Nona. The envelope also contained cruise tickets. Enough tickets, in fact, to send Alex and her Spruce Street neighbors on a cruise that was headed for an unknown destination and with a puzzle for Alex to solve.

Who is Henrietta?

SURPRISE CRUISE

"I really think I should go with you," Hawk, a private investigator and friend, said into the phone.

"I will be fine. What is the worst that can happen on a cruise ship?" Alex asked with as much bravado as she could muster.

"You could be stuck on board with a hit man, that's what, Alex! You need to take this seriously."

His words cut her to the quick. Those were the exact words she'd used during one of her last conversations with Nona, just days before she died.

"I am. I know you are concerned, but I can take care of myself."

"I know you are capable. That doesn't mean I worry any less."

"It's not necessary. You vetted the ship as best you could. The ship has its own security personnel. It will be fine," Alex replied.

She wasn't sure if she was trying to convince him or herself that everything would be fine on a week-long adventure aboard the *Tranquility* with most of her Spruce Street neighbors.

"How are we looking, Alex?" Celia asked, sitting across from Alex in her pink silk blouse and gray pencil skirt—as fabulous as ever.

Celia didn't appear flustered at all, not like Alex was looking and feeling in her oversized sweatshirt and yoga pants.

"I like what you're doing with your hair these days," Celia teased.

Alex knew Celia was eyeing the bird's nest of wavy locks atop her head. She'd piled her hair in a messy bun before rushing out of the house this morning. This was her only chance to finish all the last-minute tasks before they left for their cruise in just two days.

"I have an appointment this afternoon at the Perfect Cut. I think I am starting to get a few white hairs. Forty-two is much too young for white hair," Alex said with a grimace and scratched at her hairline. "Probably all this pressure."

Celia chuckled. "*I* wouldn't know," she said with a genuine smile and ran her hand down her immaculately straight layered bob. Her hair—the golden hue of honey pouring from a bottle—was also the perfect color from root to tip. Unlike Alex's currently fading cocoa color.

"I can't believe leaving my career in New York City was easier than coming home to Spruce Street." Alex slumped in her chair. "My stress level is through the roof. I need a vacation from this vacation, and we haven't even left yet."

Celia eyed her compassionately. "I understand. It must be hard for you. Are you sure you don't want Hawk to join us? It wouldn't hurt any to have him along. I can still book him a suite."

"Why does everyone keep asking me that?" Alex exclaimed.

"I am capable of taking care of myself without the assistance of someone of the male persuasion."

Celia put her hands up in defense. "Okay. Let's go through the list. Is everyone ready to go?"

"Well, we knew Alastor would give us trouble. He is a hard 'no,' although I have decided to leave Kibbles with him. It'll do Alastor some good. Maybe his heart will grow three sizes while we're gone."

They both had a good laugh.

Alex composed herself and wiped her eyes dry with her sleeve. "He wasn't happy about it, but I have a groomer on standby to board the pup in case he really can't handle it."

"Are you sure that curmudgeon is capable of caring for the dog?" Celia asked.

"He is the only neighbor who is home all of the time. Everyone else is just too busy."

"Well, he can't be any worse than the dog's previous owner. You really are a saint, adopting the dog of the woman who killed Nona and then tried to kill you." Celia shuddered.

"Honestly, that's what Nona would have done, don't you think?"

"Yes, I agree." Celia placed her hand on Alex's arm. Alex covered Celia's hand with her own and gave a gentle squeeze. "All right, so who *is* coming?"

"It looks like just you, Charlotte and I, Pete and Lucy."

"Betty?" Celia asked.

"Oh, yes, of course."

"How do you think she will manage without being able to bake for a week? Did she get her pie orders all straightened out?"

"You know Betty. She threatened bodily harm to anyone who would even think about going elsewhere for a pie. She's monopolized pie distribution so much that the Pop and Shop doesn't even carry pies anymore."

"How is she handling Nona's death? It mustn't be easy to lose her best friend after all these years."

"Oh, she's been more meddlesome than ever lately. She means well, even though she can be quite the busybody. I just grin and bear it. Truth is, if you listen, you can usually find some good, need-to-know facts mixed in all the gossip."

Celia shuffled some papers on her desk and checked the clock.

"How about you? Are you all set, Celia? You must be glad to be getting away."

"Oh, you know me. I have everything all set. My last client is coming in about fifteen minutes. I have three houses to show. Then, I am off duty for twenty-four hours before we get set to leave. There's nothing pressing here in Salem that can't wait a week."

"All right, I'll let you get back to it. I have to get a few things done before heading to my hair appointment." Alex grimaced again, remembering those pesky white hairs.

As she was packing her suitcase the next day, Alex couldn't help but be reminded of the events of the past few months. Alex had no regrets about leaving behind her career at the law firm Weitz & Romano. After a decade of living in New York City, she had been ready to go home to Massachusetts, though she'd thought Spruce Street was going to be a new chapter. She yearned for the simple pace of life caring for Nona. Instead of repose and welcoming arms, Alex had driven home to find mayhem .and then murder.

Then a cruise. Surprise, Alex!

It was all Alex and Celia could do to organize the entire neighborhood for the cruise these last few weeks. Alex shook her head laughing to herself. Nona had grand plans. That was for sure. *Has an entire neighborhood of residents ever taken a cruise together before?*

She picked up the picture from the top of her dresser and stroked the glass. She didn't hang onto many mementos or have a lot of *stuff*. Besides her quilts—the princess quilt her mom had made her and her graduation quilt that Nona had left for her—she had very few sentimental belongings. Of course, she had all of her own quilting supplies.

The double frame housed an image of her parents and also one of Alex and Nona. The images filled her with regrets. Of course, the loss of her parents pained her, but the years had dulled the pain. The absence of Nona, the woman who had been like a grandmother to her, was a fresh wound in Alex's heart and the circumstances of her death were regretful. Nona had gotten too close to learning about the attempt on Alex's life. A suspicion which had led to Nona's murder.

Nona had been Alex's childhood neighbor, and Alex had grown up idolizing her, even calling her grandmother. Nona had been Alex's biggest supporter. As a young girl, Alex had thought Nona was a secret ninja spy. That was until she had been old enough to realize that people with huge personalities were just that—people with huge personalities.

Alex had been especially on edge the last few days, so it was no surprise when her phone vibrated in her back pocket and she nearly jumped out of her skin.

Hawk. She pressed the call button to answer.

"I hope you're not calling to try to convince me you should be coming with us?" she teased him.

"No, no. I am headed out for a case. A real estate mogul wants me to look into some threats his wife has received."

5

"Should be interesting. A day in the life of a private investigator," she joked. "Maybe I should think about that as a second career."

"We'd make a great team," Hawk responded.

Don't I know it. They had worked nearly fifty cases together in the past for the law firm and had just spent the last few months getting close while working Nona's murder case.

"What's up, then?" she asked him.

"I finished looking into all of the passengers and crew, the ones I could get access to, anyway. I would feel much better being on board but we've done our due diligence. I didn't find any connections to the firm. No connection to the Las Vegas Rays, either. Most of their crew went to jail when Lilith ratted them all out trying to save her own skin." He paused. "For me personally, I stopped taking cases when you left. I don't think I raised any red flags since I mostly worked on your cases anyhow. I am not taking any chances though."

Lilith, also known as Jennifer, had infiltrated their small community in an ill-fated attempt to carry out a hit on Alex. Alex and Hawk suspected Alex's old firm had arranged the hit. Alex speculated that over the decade she had worked there, she must have accumulated some knowledge, possibly about a case or the firm itself, that was dangerous. However, despite their working the case diligently since Nona's death, they'd come up empty at every turn. The firm's roots were deep and veiled. Alex and Hawk knew they just had to keep pulling on each thread, and eventually, something would unravel.

"Thank you. I know you are concerned, but I will be fine."

"Okay. I'll say no more, Lex," Hawk said, using his pet name for her. "Don't forget the card. That should get you in. I had to call in some pretty big favors to get that."

"It is already in my travel bag," she assured him, looking across her bedroom at the half-filled suitcase.

The fact that he was being cautious about his choice of words reminded her that phones were never safe, despite this being her third burner in as many months. Even though Hawk and Officer Mark weren't taking any chances with her safety, she suspected that if Hawk had managed to get access to a master key card that would get her into any room aboard the ship, with few exceptions, someone else might just be able to get such access as well.

"Look, I am catching a flight in a couple hours. Call me if you need anything," he said seriously.

"Thank you. I will be fine. I'll see you when I get back."

"Later, Lex."

Alex disconnected the call and set the phone down on her dresser.

Leading up to the group's departure, Alex was as prepared for the adventure as she was ever going to be, even though she had never set foot on a cruise ship before. Not because she didn't have the means, but because her parents hadn't died in just any typical accident. They'd died on board a cruise ship.

Alex sat in her reading chair and checked on the envelope—tickets, letters, and keys. She was still uneasy about the whole adventure. Even though this ship was much smaller and the trip would be more intimate, it didn't help to quell her unrest. After the unexpected death of the former self-appointed matriarch of Spruce Street, Alex felt badly that she hadn't been able to completely fulfill Nona's last wish. Though Celia had expertly handled all of the travel logistics, little more than half of the group was joining her on the cruise.

Along with the letters and tickets, there had also been two keys in the envelope that Nona had left for Alex—a grimy old skeleton key like the one Alex's parents had used to open the turret room in her childhood home and an ordinary house key.

Of course, the keys didn't open that door or any of the doors at number 1. That had been the first thing Alex had tried when she got home from Celia's office. In fact, in the months leading up to the cruise, Alex had searched the house's other doors and had even checked the closets for hidden boxes and secret panels.

Further trying to make sense of the situation, Alex had even searched number 9, Jack's house, where Nona had lived before moving into Alex's house. Finding no matching locks there either, she even went as far as to search all of the houses on Spruce Street, including that of Alastor Arnold, the neighborhood grinch at number 3. Now *that* had been like trying to get a teenager to hand over their cell phone.

The only house she hadn't searched was number 13, which she couldn't get into. In the past few months, no one had met or even seen the new owner, Clay, the son of Martha and Roger, long-time residents who had just recently headed south to enjoy their retirement. As such, she had no luck resolving the puzzle of the two keys.

Alex rubbed her fingers over the two keys before reluctantly slipping them back inside the envelope. She tucked the envelope between the folds of the quilt, Henrietta. She didn't know where else to look for now, but she wasn't giving up on finding the secrets that the keys unlocked.

2

DON'T FORGET

Making one last sweep of the house, Alex chuckled, thinking back on the months leading up to the cruise. Celia was going to need a vacation *from* the residents, not *with* them!

Alex reached into the folds of the quilt, Henrietta, neatly packed in her carry-on bag, and felt for the envelope containing her travel documents and the two keys. It was at least the tenth time she'd checked to make sure she was all set before heading outside to meet Joey, the barista from the Rise and Grind Café, and Celia. After all, it was not like they could turn around and go back for something she forgot, and lately, it was very like her *to forget something*.

She stepped out onto the extra wide porch, set her suitcase and carry-on bag carefully on the swing, and turned to lock the oversized oak door. Locking her doors was something she was used to doing in New York but not here on Spruce Street. Until the mayhem and murder, no one ever locked their doors. Alex had taken to locking number 1 since then, but it was still unsettling.

With the sun high in the sky and a chilly breeze in the air, Alex and her neighbors left their houses. She caught sight of

Alastor from number 3, who was just heading to Rise and Grind Café to meet his cronies for afternoon coffee. It hadn't been long after the invitations had been announced that Alex had finally given up pestering Alastor to come along and decided it was best to leave him in charge of the neighborhood. Okay, maybe just best to *leave* him. The *in charge* part she still wasn't sure about.

"My brother's coming. He'll be here to help me keep a watchful eye on the neighborhood," Alastor had said to Alex before impolitely telling her where to go, and it wasn't back to number 1! And she had serious reservations about leaving Kibbles with him too.

What could happen in seven days? Alex shuddered at the thought. Just a few months ago, murder had happened in a time span not much greater.

She had dropped Kibbles off at Alastor's the day before to give them time to acclimate and give her time to call for an emergency pet sitter. Kibbles hadn't taken to Alastor, but Alex hoped she would get used to him quickly. *I'm still trying to figure out how I ended up with a killer's dog in the first place!*

Number 1 stood atop of a rolling hill that gave view to all the neighbors and their houses on the crescent-shaped cul-de-sac. Alex's neighbors strolled their luggage down their driveways to their respective sidewalks, a few of which were still the original cobblestones from the formation of the neighborhood.

The shuttle bus arrived right on time to pick up the funny bunch, starting with Alex, Celia, and Joey. Joey had arrived at Alex's just a few minutes prior to the shuttle, a little bed-worn with his hair matted flat to the side of his head. Alex smiled as he handed her a hot chocolate, no whipped cream—her standard order and favorite indulgence.

The recent daily orders of hot chocolate from the Rise and Grind Café were creeping up on her waistline. She had gained several pounds since moving back to Spruce Street. She didn't complain, though. This morning's hot chocolate was a sweet gesture, and Alex was more than grateful for the little shots of caffeine that Joey had been adding to her hot chocolate in the past week. It was a small help to bolster her self-confidence leading up to the departure.

As Alex took the first step to board the shuttle bus, she steeled herself for what was surely going to be a long night. She chose the first seat on the left, opposite Joey and Celia and just behind the driver. One by one, the shuttle picked up each of the remaining residents: Charlotte, Betty, and Pete and Lucy from number 11, who boarded last before the bus left the suburb and headed for the city. From Boston, they would catch their nonstop flight to Florida before boarding the cruise ship *Tranquility* just after 7 p.m.

Alex started to doze off, staring out the window, watching the evening traffic flowing into the city.

As if the cruise wasn't over the top enough, Nona had arranged for a private jet to take the group to the cruise ship. *No lines, no waiting at the large international airport,* Alex thought as she and her neighbors simply boarded the jet and flew off to Florida. After a bit of stomach-lurching turbulence, Alex and her friends were at the cruise line terminal and in the security line to board the ship in just under four hours.

"Do not put your passports in your luggage." Celia reiterated the message she had repeated at least a dozen times in the days leading up to the cruise and again on the shuttle ride as well. "They should be in your carry-on bag. Everyone, please, please make sure. Once they take the luggage, that's it. You won't be able to get to it for quite a while, and you won't be able to board the ship without your paperwork."

Standing in line to go through the X-ray machine and have their carry-ons scanned, Alex wiped at the sweat beading on her forehead. She squeezed her bag under her arm. Henrietta was safely tucked away with the two keys and her passport and travel documents. She still felt compelled to unzip the bag and check, one last time.

In front of her, Pete wore the ugliest Hawaiian shirt she had ever seen. He'd traded in his retirement outfit—work shirt and overalls—for a beach bum look. *No handyman required here.* Although Alex was sure he would find something to fix. He always did. He stood beside his wife, Lucy, who was the town's clerk.

Pete held his hand out to usher Lucy forward and shouldered her bag. Pete hung back a few steps and appraised her from behind. *Retired but not dead*, Alex thought with a grin as the group shuffled into the terminal building.

At the head of the pack, Betty had a firm grip on Joey's arm. She had taken up the business of *trying* to be the grandmother to the group since Nona's death, and it wasn't working. *She's better suited to her pie-making business. According to Nona, I am responsible for the neighborhood now. In truth, no one is going to be able to fill her shoes.*

Alex passed Celia, who stood off to the side and kept watch over each person as they made their way into the check-in station, which was roped off ahead. After everyone had gone through, Celia filed into the short priority line behind Alex.

"I hope you will relax while we are cruising," Alex said to Celia.

"Once we get on board . . . and to our cabins . . . and everyone gets settled." Celia flashed a hopeful smile. "The ship has their own staff, the equivalent of me, on board."

The ship was lit up like a Christmas tree on Christmas Eve. All was dark on the horizon, save for thousands of twinkling lights dotting the ramp, the decks, and cabin windows.

The group made their way through the short line, answering the questions, filling out the required paperwork, and having their picture taken for security. A Windsom staff member handed Alex her cruise card, a schedule, and a map. Then, they all followed the signs to the gangway.

The ship was too long for Alex to see its entire length, but she could see its name decal on the side. Approaching the gangway, she stopped briefly to watch the hustle below. The men on foot and in forklifts momentarily mesmerized her, moving about loading the ship with all the necessities—pallets of food and beverages, paper goods, and flowers and greenery. Unmarked crates sparked her imagination. *What else is being loaded?*

Joey bumped into her. "Sorry, Alex. I was caught up watching." He pointed to the men below.

"No worries. Me too."

She laughed and looked fondly at the young barista she had grown to deeply care for over the last few months. Nona had adopted him into their family, and Alex now cared for him as the little brother she'd never had.

"Let's go." She waved him on. "Let's get this over with."

She gripped her bag close, eyeing another photographer just ahead. She had to smile at the comedic nature of Pete's and Lucy's image and then was instantly reminded of the photo of her parents. They likely would have stood on a similar gangway, posing in their own tourist trap. She retreated further into her hoodie and frowned.

"Smile," the woman behind the camera said.

Alex looked up, and the shutter clicked repeatedly.

Joey laughed. "You should see your face, Alex. Those pictures are going to be funny."

"Ha, ha. She could have at least waited for me to compose myself."

"I think that was the point." Joey nudged her playfully.

3

COCKTAILS

THE GROUP ENTERED THE SHIP ON WHAT ALEX THOUGHT was the fifth deck, arriving in a large atrium with enormous chandeliers overhead. Finally on board, she and her neighbors were free to explore the upper decks and amenities for a short time. A calming voice played various announcements over the loudspeakers. According to the omniscient voice from above, their cabins would be ready by 6:30 p.m. and muster, whatever that was, was at 7 p.m. sharp.

Biting her lip, Alex looked at her watch. Just a half hour to go before she could escape to her cabin, even if just briefly. She smoothed her hair and patted her shoulder bag again.

Alex walked up to the bartender at the tiki hut and nodded. "I will have one of these," she said, holding up a small drink card advertising a cocktail called Rising Tides. The card depicted a drink the color of orange sherbet presented in a frosted glass. The ingredients listed: vodka, lime, orange, and watermelon juice, finished with a cucumber wheel.

"Getting your fruits and veggies all in one?" The bartender shared a wide, bright smile and waited long enough for her to nod before walking away to prepare her beverage.

As she sat on the barstool, she remembered the ship's brochure in her back pocket. She took it out and unfolded the pamphlet. Coincidentally, it did not foretell anything about their destination but detailed the ship's features. She read: *Tranquility, voted World's Best Small Ship–Cruise Ship*. Classified as a small ship–cruise ship, there was nothing small about it at 525 feet long, which according to the brochure was the equivalent of two city blocks; nearly as long as the Washington Monument is tall, or about half the length of a typical cruise ship. Alex devoured every detail. As a defense attorney, she was all too aware that the devil was in the details.

The brochure boasted the ship had *all the comforts of home*. With only a 312-passenger capacity but a 195-person crew, there was nearly one staff member for every one and a half guests, and according to the brochure, the ship wasn't lacking any of the traditional amenities typically found on the larger cruise ships. Rounding out the amenities were a spa, salon, pool, and a hot tub.

Alex's eyes were immediately drawn to a clever marketing trick. All the key descriptive words were ever so slightly bolder —*unwind, luxurious, soothing* and so on. To an untrained eye, the difference would be indiscernible.

Alex could only hope for the ability to unwind. It had been one thing after another lately. First, she'd left the law firm. Then, Nona had been killed, and then there'd been an attempt on her own life. After all that, Alex was wound tighter than Betty's curlers.

The gang joined her at the bar, and a few Rising Tides later, Alex was fulfilling her only agenda for the week—to relax and enjoy herself—when the omniscient voice announced the passengers were free to head to their cabins.

"Let's grab Joey and Pete," Celia said. She led them back to the deck tables nearest the elevator. Rather than waiting, Celia steered the group to a nearby stairwell.

At the top of the short flight of steps, Celia stood holding the door open and waved them out of the stairwell and into the corridor. She gave a Vanna White wave toward the left wall, where a large number six was bolted to the wall, as well as a cork display board that read *Welcome Aboard*. To the right was a long corridor with a set of glass doors at the end.

"This way." She led the group down the corridor to their block of rooms.

"Look to your right as we walk by," she said.

Alex and Joey glanced to their right, and Celia chuckled. She had put up a temporary sign that said *Spruce Street*.

In fact, Celia had put up several fun little signs, temporarily labeling the cabins. She had changed the cabin numbers to reflect the residents' house numbers. Number 11 for Pete and Lucy, number 7 for Betty, and number 1 for Alex. Sure enough, just like on Spruce Street, all the rooms were out of order and also only on the left, on the port side of the hall.

"Nona," Alex said under her breath, though the embellishment made her smile.

Joey stood at his door, number 2, on the right just across from Alex's cabin. Even though he was a boy to Alex, he was a full-fledged adult in college, and like her, this was his first cruise. She could see the trepidation hiding behind a mask of excitement.

I'll keep an eye on him. Although Alex had tried to get to know Joey and make him feel welcome, he was about to embark on a weeklong journey with a boat full of people he barely knew. He was a sweet, fresh-faced young man, talkative and not shy at all. Lanky but handsome, his sandy blond hair that shagged across his chocolate-brown eyes. She had only known Joey a few months. First as the courteous barista at the café, when she came back to Spruce Street, then as someone Nona had chosen to adopt into her life. Finding out that Nona was paying for his tuition, at Nona's celebration of life, hadn't really come as a shock to Alex.

Alex endeavored to continue Nona's good works. It was thanks to Nona he was getting a free ride to college, but in reality, it was Alex's parents who had made possible everything that Alex and Nona had been able to accomplish over the years. Alex's parents had had the foresight to acquire overly healthy life insurance policies. Added to the payout from the cruise line for the *accident*, the life insurance benefits ensured that neither Alex nor Nona had to worry about money, and neither did Joey, now.

She looked at him. "If you need anything..." She put her hand to her ear, miming a phone. "I will see you in thirty minutes for muster."

4

MUSTER

ALEX LOOKED AROUND AT THE WELL-APPOINTED *WINDSOM Cruise Line* accommodations. Her room was enormous, considering what she had expected. The walls were a soft calming shade of greige. The suite had two areas—the bedroom and a small sitting area with a small love seat for two and a comfy chair—three areas if she counted the balcony. All of the furnishings were navy trimmed with rich gold. Beyond the love seat, a sheer curtain covered the door to the balcony. The queen-sized bed had no less than four layers of pillows, two layers of sleeping pillows in crisp white cases with navy trim and then one layer of throws and one layer of round bolster pillows. She squeezed one of the sleeping pillows to see if it was as soft as it looked. Her fingers sank into the pillow, the fluffy material poofing around them like clouds.

Alex turned, scanning the suite's lavish appointments, and walked to the mini fridge, almost catching her shin on the edge of the bed. She was parched. She didn't drink alcohol very often, especially not in that short amount of time nor on an empty stomach. Alex opened the mini fridge door, looking for a bottle of water. Inside, she found water . . . and a fully stocked minibar, and made a mental note to remove the liquor from Joey's room if Celia hadn't already taken care of it.

She uncapped the bottle and found relief from the thirst brought on by two too many cocktails. A flat screen TV hung at eye level. Though it was nice, she couldn't imagine how much television anyone actually watched with all there was to do on the ship.

Next to the fridge sat a small table and a three ring binder. Alex absently rifled through the binder and papers on the table—agendas, a map, and a welcome letter. She turned to investigate the bathroom. A pair of slippers sat by the tub just inside the door. Eyeing the small stand-up shower, she wondered what the water pressure was like. *No time for a shower. We have muster in less than a half hour.* The sleek granite sink had an oversized mirror and a ledge for bottles and jars. An origami towel bowl full of L' Best amenities sat to one side. *That must've cost a small fortune to appoint all the rooms with.*

Alex knew exactly how much Nona had paid for the trip. Though the money had come from the joint bank account Alex had set up for Nona, it was Nona's. Hers to be spent however she saw fit. To be used for living expenses, fun money, and to help the neighborhood. Though Nona had thought it was worth it, Alex wasn't sure of the extravagant expense and only time would tell.

Alex shivered and turned back into the living area to search for the thermostat and turned the temperature from sixty-five to seventy degrees.

She stared mesmerized as the curtains billowed. It was like the ocean was calling to her. Curious, she stepped out onto her tiny private balcony overlooking the Atlantic. The cool night air gave her a chill. She envisioned a mirage of a tropical island destination from a romance movie, with stars overhead and the moon shining bright, waves crashing ashore, and a small rowboat roped to a lone palm tree.

The speakers boomed overhead, announcing muster, and a simultaneous knock on the door snapped her from the ocean's lure. She moved back through the room and opened the door. In the corridor, her neighbors were filing out of their own rooms, herding to the left toward the end of the hall. Other passengers passed her, going to the right in the opposite direction. Alex nearly bumped into a heavyset man in a fedora.

"Excuse me. My apologies," she said.

Her stomach dropped as she scanned his appearance. The fedora perched on his round face caught her off guard. It reminded her of Remo Romano, one of the two partners at her old law firm in New York. A chill ran down her spine. Though they had not yet been able to prove the law firm had taken out the hit on her, she knew it to be the truth, deep down in her gut.

The tall, slender redhead behind him stopped short on his heels. "My, my, what trouble are you causing now, husband?" She playfully swatted at him from behind.

"Ma'am." He tipped his fedora toward Alex, and she nodded in response.

The redhead reached for the man's gloved hand. The two bantered back and forth as they scuttled away in the opposite direction.

"Come, now, you big oaf," the woman said, teasing the man.

"Listen, woman, if you call me an oaf one more time!" he said, and his bellowing laughter filled the corridor behind Alex.

"Let's find Arthur," Alex thought the woman said before their voices finally trailed off.

Alex mused at the curious companionable banter between the two and peered down the hallway just as Pete and Lucy popped out of their room, looking more than a little disheveled. *They couldn't have, in such a short time? No . . . Probably!* She laughed as they giggled behind her. Maybe this cruise just might be fun after all. She had to hand it to Pete. Despite being ten years older than Lucy, he still had his mojo.

As it turned out, muster was held in a private lounge for the Spruce Street gang. A space they would have to themselves for the remainder of the trip, except during the quilting class times or if there should be an emergency.

Inside the lounge, various signs proclaimed *No Food or Drink During Muster*. Alex was getting increasingly peckish. All she'd had was the hot chocolate Joey had brought her when they had left and a half a sandwich on the plane hours ago. None of which comprised a proper meal, especially after cocktails.

Ten minutes later—although it seemed like forever—the meeting finally got underway. The crew members gave a safety briefing explaining the different alarms. Three long alarms for man overboard, or MOB as they called it, continuous for fire, and seven short and one long for the general alarm, though they didn't explain what constituted a general alarm. What Alex keyed in on was that the captain would give verbal instructions with the general alarm should there be a necessity to abandon ship.

Gooseflesh erupted across her entire body at the thought, and she trembled for an instant, thinking of her parents standing in a meeting similar to this, unaware of any danger they would later face. The details of her parents' death were sparse, and she preferred not to dwell on it. Though, over the years, there had been times when she had been driven to find answers. Most of her anxiety had been quelled by Nona.

"It was a tragic accident. Dwelling on things out of our control won't help. It is best to leave well enough alone," Nona would say to Alex.

Standing there, Alex fought the grief bubbling under the

surface of the calm controlled exterior that she had worked so hard to cultivate over the years. *Maybe it is time to let Hawk investigate the accident.* Alex was deep in thought when the demonstration ended with a show on how to properly don a life jacket.

Once muster had concluded, the whole group hung back with Celia while the remainder of the passengers dispersed. The gang was led out onto the private balcony, where they could order food and drinks before watching the ship set sail. On the open-air deck, Alex felt the lure of the ocean once again and the peace and tranquility that it brought. Not even the sight of the emergency lifeboats ready and waiting on the deck could disrupt the serenity of the ocean. It was like they were in a bubble and had the ship to themselves now.

Celia introduced everyone to Jane, who would be in charge of a small group of staff dedicated to serving the gaggle of Spruce Street residents.

"We hit the jackpot with Jane. She will be here to answer questions and get you where you need to go. If you need anything at all, you just let her know," Celia said and stepped aside, giving Jane the floor.

Jane quickly introduced herself and each of the waitstaff. She seemed nice enough, but Alex couldn't help thinking Jane looked upset, like someone who had just received bad news or whose plans had suddenly changed.

Alex was distracted from Jane's spiel by the clinking and clattering of the waitstaff loading the buffet behind her. The aroma of warm bread wafted in the air, and her mouth watered.

Pete came up beside her and pointed to Jane. "She has killer legs."

Alex laughed, and then her stomach growled fiercely.

She surveyed the outdoor space. The deck was large enough for a bar, plus the buffet, three full-size round banquet tables, seating by the railing, and plenty of room to move around. The small group of seven sat together, squeezing in at just one table. Joey sat to Alex's right and Celia to her left. She smiled in appreciation of the table adornments. The fine linen and crystal glasses reminded her of dinner parties her parents used to have when she had been a young girl.

Alex watched as Joey's eyes darted back and forth between multiple pieces of silverware and winked at him. "Eat with whatever fork you want to. There's no silverware police here!"

His shoulders relaxed. "Thank you. This is much fancier than I expected," he said, looking down at his khaki pants and polo T-shirt.

They all had been required to bring certain dress clothes, so she knew he was prepared. He had told her that his parents had taken him shopping before the trip.

"You are fine. I will remind you when you have to dress up," she said and waved at her own casual attire with a flourish.

Joey smiled.

Alex admired the purple flower garnish on the plates. To her surprise, the server gave a lesson on dining etiquette and the proper use of the silverware before a chef began grilling table-side. She would have been perfectly happy with just a buffet, but with a buffet *and* grilled steaks, she was in heaven. The smoky aroma filled the air as she listened to the chatter of her friends and loved ones as they set sail on their adventure.

No one was disappointed with the rich foods. Alex was full after the exquisite meal. She wanted nothing more than to change into her pajamas and curl up under a quilt. On the short walk back to her cabin, she passed a member of the staff with an empty luggage cart and was reminded of her luggage. She pressed her key card to the door and waited for the beep to signify the door had unlocked. Inside, her luggage stood neatly beside her bed, and she sighed in relief. There was something comforting about having all her belongings with her.

She was no stranger to being away from home. After all, between college and the near decade she'd worked at the law firm, she had lived in New York for nearly twenty years. This trip, this vacation was unusual for Alex. As a kid, she'd never vacationed. She'd always stayed home while her parents had cruised. As an adult, her vacations consisted mostly of her trips home to Spruce Street for the holidays.

Alex looked around the suite for a place to store the luggage, deciding under the bed was the only suitable space. Everything was so finely appointed that she was grateful Celia had made her buy new luggage and that she hadn't brought one of her hand-me-down pieces or her old duffle bag. Even though she had the means to live more lavishly, she chose to be frugal. *Waste not, want not,* as the old saying went. In this gorgeous room, she couldn't imagine leaving the luggage or her clothes all over the place, so she unpacked her clothes, shaking out the wrinkles. She hung her sundresses and refolded her casuals, putting her personal items into the drawers.

Bending to tuck the luggage under the bed, she could see her carry-on sitting on the floor where she had tucked it under the overhanging comforter earlier. Alex pulled the bag from underneath the bed and gave it a squeeze, remembering the quilt, Henrietta, was still inside. She unzipped the bag and ran her hand across the textures of the fabric and quilting. Giving this quilt away was going to be bittersweet. On the one hand, she was anxious to know who Henrietta was and get a glimpse into Nona's secret life. On the other hand, it was hard to give up such an important piece of Nona.

She pushed aside the curtain and looked out the glass

balcony door. Thankfully, Nona had had the sense to order them all modest balcony suites and not the grand suites. The balcony was just large enough for some potted greenery—a hosta or maybe some kind of ground cover plant—and a seat. She sat in the small deck chair and thought back on her attempts to garden; she had given it the old college try before resorting to Nona's suggestion of hiring landscapers.

"And the yard never looked so good!" Nona's words echoed in her mind, and she smiled fondly at the memory.

With so many unanswered questions surrounding who was after her and where Nona was taking them on this trip, Alex's heart was still heavy with concern. Alex dropped her shoulders and relaxed as she sat back against the chair. It was not at all comfortable, so she went inside and closed the sliding door. She left the curtains open and opted for the love seat rather than the bed just yet. It was better than the deck chair but not nearly as comfortable as the stuffed pig, the hideous love seat back home. The one Nona had purchased to Alex's dismay but had turned out to be the most comfortable seat in the house.

Alex lay back and stared out into the night sky. The moon was bright and almost full. She could see all of the craters and colorations. They all trusted Nona but Alex couldn't help but wonder *where* they were going, which led to her thinking about Nona. Pondering how Nona had mysteriously called Alex home, for one, and all of her uncharacteristic and oddball behaviors, like spying on her neighbors. It was the secret double life that troubled Alex as she sat there staring out into the dark of night. What had begun as a mother's upset about her son's unexpected marriage had ended with her murder. Was it the fullness of the moon that amplified Alex's doubt and regrets? Maybe if Alex, or Officer Mark, could have caught the killer sooner or if Nona had been more forthcoming with the truth, she would be here with Alex on this trip.

Then, there were the mystery quilts Nona had left, labeled Henrietta, Liam, and Rebecca Briggs. The problem of there being no last name for the quilt labeled Liam, and search results in the tens of thousands for the name Rebecca Briggs, left Alex unsettled.

In front of her, a small, rectangular wooden bench served as a coffee table, decorated with a single plant in an ornate pot. Alex did not know what kind of plant it was. Tall with purple flowers, it was much the same as the flowers garnishing the plates at dinnertime. *Exotic,* she thought. She leaned forward and checked but didn't find a marker.

Sitting back, she closed her eyes and quickly fell asleep. In her dreams, the scenes of the day played back in slow motion, a soft haze blurring the edges. She woke up warm and content sometime in the middle of the night. Not bothering to change into her pajamas, she tucked herself into the luxurious bed and was quickly asleep again.

5

DAY ONE

In the morning, Alex decided to shower and trade her comfy pants for a pair of cotton shorts. Paying little attention to how she looked, she threw on a tank top that didn't match and strapped on a pair of flat, open-toed sandals to finish her casual ensemble. A quick look at the ship's activities showed her options of exploring the boat, lounging by the pool, and gambling at the casino, plus movies, a skydiving simulator, a craft-beer tasting in the yacht club, and a napkin-folding class. The latter she thought might actually be fun. She was grateful for the planned afternoon of quilting.

Alex made her way to Joey's room before the 8 a.m. group breakfast and knocked on his door. When he didn't answer, she assumed that he was already in the lounge.

Alex caught a sleepy nod from Charlotte as she entered the lounge. Everyone including Joey was already seated or making their way through the breakfast buffet. She nodded to Joey as she walked up to the breakfast line herself. The offerings were hearty, with scrambled eggs, bacon, ham and sausage, pancakes and waffles, beans, grits, biscuits and gravy, and a variety of breakfast breads and muffins. The buffet tables were decorated with fresh fruit displays as well as the usual continental items.

Who is supposed to eat all this food? There is enough food to feed the entire ship. There's only seven of us!

Before everyone left for the day, Celia encouraged the Spruce Street flock to join her on deck 8 at a posh restaurant and lounge, known as the Yacht Club. A place for luncheons, including a mingles lunch starting at noon, with the other passengers. Being that this was the first cruise for all of them, they agreed to follow Celia's agenda, which was likely an order from Nona anyway.

Back in her luxurious suite, Alex lingered on her balcony for a few hours, most of which time she spent fidgeting up and down in her lounge chair. The railing on the balcony was at just the wrong height to get a clear view of the ocean scenery. She either had to scrunch down to see through the glass panel or stretch her neck to see above the railing.

After a quick change into something less beachy, Alex left the room mildly agitated and not at all in the right frame of mind for a "mingles lunch." She scowled at the thought. *I am so bad at meeting people who don't need a lawyer.* To her, conversations were just another form of interrogation. Sometimes, she found it hard to include the extra pleasantries and social etiquette needed to make conversation.

She met up with Joey at the elevator. As they stood waiting, Joey nodded to the wall. Alex stepped closer to a framed cork board that had dozens of pictures attached to it now.

"See, I told you this would be a funny picture. Look at the face you made when the photographer took our picture," he said, laughing.

She scanned the pictures of mostly couples and executives, many of whom had the same facial expression that she did—which wasn't at all funny because she was going to have to see it every time she came to this elevator. In the center of all of the photographs was Pete's and Lucy's, and Alex smiled at the silliness of their poses.

"Pete's a funny guy, don't you think, Alex?" Joey pointed to the picture Alex had her eye on.

"He sure is!"

On the far right was the happy Italian family, the husband and wife with her flaming red hair and their son.

"They must have put them up just before muster," Joey said as the elevator chimed and the doors opened.

Neither spoke on the quick ride up to deck 8. Joey's fidgeting told her he didn't want to go to the mingles lunch any more than she did.

They stepped off the elevator. Everyone else was in their semiformal daytime attire. Alex glanced down at her dress pants, grateful she had changed out of her shorts. The other guests had an air of wealth about them. Though Alex was wealthy, she didn't put it on display. She had nice things but chose a more modest look over one of extravagance. Alex had worked all her life because Nona had told her she needed a career and something to labor at.

Her Spruce Street neighbors seemed less out of place as she felt. Alex weaved through the groupings of passengers with Joey behind her. She eyed a few couples of retirement age and older businessmen still donning suits and ties. The entire crowd was at least twenty years her senior, except for the woman from the hallway earlier. Her extraordinary red hair wouldn't be missed in any crowd. Alex estimated the woman to be in her late forties, though her husband—who was very much Italian, with dark brown hair and olive skin and was now sporting a different fedora—appeared to be in his early sixties. With them a young man of Joey's age. If it wasn't obvious by the shaggy red mop of hair, then it was clear by the way the woman fussed over him, that he was their son. *Well, at least there is one person Joey's age . . . and a few people my age, if I count Charlotte, Celia, and this woman.*

Alex turned to Joey. "I think his name is Arthur." She nodded in the trio's direction. "Let's do this!" she said with a deep breath, urging him to follow her.

At least she didn't have to go it alone. She laughed at the thought of being Joey's wingman. She hadn't ever been a twenty-year-old's sidekick before.

The party wasn't making the tension headache slowly building across her forehead any better. She rolled her shoulders to release the tightness in her back. Instead of mingling she made a beeline for the bar. Luckily, as she was ordering sodas for herself and Joey, Arthur came straight for Joey, followed by his parents. As the two twentysomethings hit it off, they moved to a nearby table, talking like they were best buds, and the parents opened up conversation with Alex.

"How old is your son?" the woman asked Alex.

"Oh, no, he's a friend of the family. A college student." Alex chuckled. She wasn't sure if she should be offended or flattered. Joey was a sweet guy, but she wasn't sure she liked the assumption that she was twice his age and old enough to be his mom, even though she was.

"I'm sorry." Arthur's mom extended her hand and teetered a bit. The woman wore a gorgeous white cocktail dress and was clearly intoxicated. Alex couldn't help but stare. The contrast of the white dress and her vivid red hair was a bit extreme, though she was an attractive woman, slender and very curvy, like Jessica Rabbit. Her eyes were wide and striking as well, despite being a bit bloodshot. To Alex, the woman looked happy, and

Alex wondered what her own eyes told strangers about her. She had never really thought about it before. She was pretty and had no problem attracting men, but did her whiskey-colored eyes convey happiness or maybe her inner longing?

"Where are your manners?" the woman asked, looking at her husband and smiling. Her grin was nearly as big as her personality.

The man harrumphed. "My name is Ernesto." He locked eyes with Alex for an uncomfortable beat.

Is he, too, searching to see what my eyes are saying?

"This is my wife, Birdie, and, of course, our son, Arthur." He pointed his scotch glass in the general direction of the young men.

Birdie added, "We are here for a fabulous family vacation, just the three of us."

Alex thought she saw Ernesto's chin quivering at his wife's words. She extended her hand to him. "I'm Alex, and that's Joey." She turned and nodded in the same direction he had.

A bit self-conscious, Alex still wasn't getting into this mingle business and she caught herself wanting to fidget. She forced herself to hold her composure through the small talk but she was anxious to get to quilting. Celia had promised there would be quilting on this cruise.

"Hours and hours of uninterrupted quilting. And the best part is that everything will be provided for you, so don't fuss," Celia had said before they left, and she had sounded just like Nona. No doubt her words were from an actual script left by Nona.

The man said something Alex missed while she was off in her own thoughts.

"Behave," the woman said to her husband, swatting him on the rump.

"I'm no monk," he responded with a devious grin.

Betty called Alex from behind.

Alex turned to greet her. "Betty," Alex said in a clipped tone. The last thing she wanted was gossip.

"Alex, are you going to introduce me to your new friends?" Betty asked.

"Betty, this is Birdie and Ernesto and their son, Arthur." Alex pointed toward Joey and Arthur again.

"What unusual names. I am a connoisseur of names . . . and pies," Betty said, and Alex frowned. *What on earth is she going on about now?*

"This is Betty Rekorc." Alex motioned toward Betty.

The man tipped his fedora to Betty. "Ma'am, pleased to meet you."

"Well, I am glad Joey will have someone his age." Betty turned to Alex. "You won't have to worry about him while we're quilting later this afternoon. You know we are scheduled for a quilt session in the private lounge?"

"Yes, and Joey is going to be joining us for quilting," Alex replied.

Nona would roll over in her grave if Alex didn't at least try to get him involved with quilting in some way. After all, quilting wasn't just for women.

Betty smirked. "Oh, that's nice. Nona would have gotten a kick out of that! I have met a few other women who are here for quilting too, and I heard there is one *man* coming." She waggled her eyebrows and turned to the redhead. "Are you a quilter, Birdie?"

"Yes."

Alex was more than a little surprised and quickly reined in her eyebrows, which had lifted without her permission.

Birdie asked, "Lounge on deck 6, right?"

Betty nodded before Alex could answer.

"I'm scheduled to be there this afternoon," Birdie stated, "while the men do some fishing."

"Not my sport, really," her husband responded. "I am more of a hunter." He winked at Alex.

She couldn't help curling her lip. The guy was a little too cheesy. No . . . sleazy. Whatever it was, she didn't like him.

"Really? A hunter!" The wife laughed. "What a thing to say. You have never hunted a thing in your life."

There it is again. His jaw twitched after Birdie spoke.

Ernesto shrugged off his wife's comment and didn't respond.

Alex frowned. She was out of sorts not having to be on guard every moment with her feelings, thoughts, and facial reactions.

"Well, it was nice to meet you both," she said. "I'm going to head back to my cabin now. Birdie, I will see you a little later."

Alex walked away, scanning the deck for Joey to let him know she was leaving.

At the table farthest from the commotion of passengers, she found the two young men engrossed in their phones.

"Joey, will you be all right to find your way back? Remember, we're meeting in the private lounge in..." She checked her watch. "Less than a half hour."

"Yes, I'll stay here a bit longer. Arthur is telling me about Pokémon hunting. Apparently, people of all ages do it." His eyes beamed with excitement. "Not just children," he added quickly. "I have never heard of it before, though, have you, Alex?"

"Yes," she said begrudgingly, thinking of all of the people crowded on the corners during tournaments. As if the New York City street corners weren't crowded enough. "Don't stay too long."

"Can Arthur have breakfast with us in the private lounge tomorrow?"

Arthur gave Alex an assured look and said, "We have cabins just down the hall from yours. My folks are in one, and I have a single across the hall, which is right next door to Joey's. My parents are fighting. I don't think my dad wanted me to come on this trip."

This statement seemed odd to Alex, as she had just been thinking about how genuinely happy Birdie looked with her husband.

She dismissed the thought. "Yes, Arthur, I'm sure that would be fine."

She felt a stitch of sympathy for him. However, the two young men quickly dismissed her and went back to their phones. Alex smiled. The two guys were going to be inseparable, she could already tell.

Alex made her way past Arthur's parents. She nodded as she passed the lively couple, and Betty broke away, following Alex to the elevator.

Deep in thought, Alex nearly bumped into Jane.

"I am sorry. I wasn't paying attention to where I was going," Alex said.

"No, it was my fault. I was preoccupied. Please, go ahead." Jane held a gift basket away from her side, backed up, and waved Alex on with her gloved hand. Jane turned and quickly walked off.

"Jane . . ." Alex called out, but Jane didn't turn back.

What was that all about?

Betty gave Alex a nudge in the direction of the elevator.

Alex jumped, startled, and put her hand to her chest. "Geez, Betty."

"What was she carrying? It looked more like a potted plant inside the wrapped basket than a gift. Did you see? Who gives someone a potted plant on a cruise ship?"

Alex stared at Betty quizzically.

Betty rocked her head back and forth in disbelief. "The card. Did you see the card, Alex? Taped to the cellophane. *To my darling wife.*"

"I don't know. Why does it matter?" Alex smiled. "You can't possibly keep track of all the gossip on a ship this size, Betty, no matter how much you'd like to."

Betty pouted for a moment. Then, she launched into a new topic, talking Alex's ear off. "Are you excited about quilting this afternoon? I wonder what quilt pattern we will work on. I hope it is not a grandmother's flower garden quilt!"

Alex cringed at the thought of working on a handwork quilt on the cruise. There was no way that would be the chosen pattern. After Nona's death, Alex had found a stack of ten quilts in Nona's stash closet, all of them grandmother's flower garden quilts—the only type of quilt Nona ever made. Several had been labeled with first names and no other identification, one of which was Henrietta, the quilt she had in her cabin. She would have to sort through and deliver them, which was why it had been her job to bring Henrietta on the cruise.

"Alex, are you listening?" Betty asked as Alex snapped out of her thoughts.

"Yes, Betty, I am sorry. What did you say?"

Alex pressed the button for the elevator, and the door opened immediately.

"I asked, are you going to have lunch at the yacht club again tomorrow for the next mingles event?"

Alex sighed. "Yes, I will go along with whatever Celia has planned for us," she said reluctantly.

What else would I do?

The elevator came to a gentle stop on deck 6, and the doors chimed and opened. Alex motioned for Betty to go first, hoping to interrupt her logorrhea.

"It's pretty exciting, if you ask me. I peeked at where we are going," Betty continued.

"Don't tell me." Alex put up her hand to stop Betty from blurting out the details.

The destination was supposed to be a mystery, and Alex was following Nona's request.

"Some of us still do not know," Alex said, putting her finger to her lips to further reiterate her point.

Sure, Alex could have easily looked at the postings in the common areas and known the destination, but she carefully averted her eyes whenever she passed. Or like now, and a few minutes ago, she just walked blindly past.

Nona wouldn't just send her friends and family on a random trip. It had to be important to Nona, and Alex would honor her wishes as best she could. Besides, they were on a thirteen-ton floating city in the middle of the Atlantic Ocean. There was no going back!

Betty prattled on. "The suites are so roomy. The fresh fruit and the flowers in the room . . . such a nice touch. This trip must have cost Nona a small fortune. I didn't even know she had that kind of money." She paused long enough for Alex to respond. In fact, sometimes the only time Betty stopped talking was when *she* wanted info.

"Speaking of suites," Alex said just in front of her cabin door. She reached for her key card. "I am going to freshen up. I'll meet you in a bit, Betty."

Alex slipped into her cabin to avoid answering Betty's gossip inquiry. She kicked off her tennis shoes, tucked them under the small side table, and retrieved a bottle of water from the mini fridge.

All the talking and thinking in the elevator had made Alex nostalgic for Nona. She bent down to pull out the luggage from under her bed, carefully unzipped the carry-on, and lifted

Henrietta out of her bag. The skeleton key tucked inside plonked on the floor, narrowly missing her little toe. Alex bent again to pick up the curious-looking key and inspected it as she sat on the bed. It was uniquely ornate, unlike any standard skeleton key she had ever seen. She vaguely remembered Nona had some strange keys. She and Nona's granddaughter, Charlotte, used to play with them. When they were kids, everything was a treasure to be explored.

Growing up, Alex always thought Nona was a bit peculiar. She had never been able to put her finger on it, even after all these years. When Nona had come to live with and care for Alex, she had acted like you would expect a grandmotherly figure to act. Nona had kept Alex busy with schoolwork, quilting, cooking, and such. Alex had always been grateful for that. It had left little time to wallow in self-pity or the grief from the loss of her parents. Raising Alex had been all business to Nona. It had been like they had just fallen into a rhythm. Nona had simply picked up where Alex's parents had left off. It had been good, but it had been as though Alex hadn't actually grieved for her parents' loss back then. Sure, she had cried and screamed from time to time, but Nona had just pulled her along to the next task or chore.

Alex hadn't realized she was gripping Henrietta so tightly in her lap that she'd wrinkled the quilt. She smoothed out the crinkled section and admired Nona's handwork, the stitches so tiny even a trained eye wouldn't see them. The quilt had been made from over two thousand small hexagons that had been molded around little cardboard templates and hand stitched together before the cardboard had been removed, making a gorgeous lap-size quilt, with a wide array of teals and aquas as the background colors and rich caramels, browns, and greens, with all the bright flower colors, in the center. It was quintessentially tropical.

She sat on the love seat and laced up her shoes. Looking around, she couldn't help thinking that she was missing something or that she ought to have her hands full of quilting supplies. Everything she needed for the quilt project would be provided for her, but she rummaged through her bag and found her date for the evening—a one-of-a-kind wooden seam ripper made by a wood turner local to New England. She smiled at the long-standing joke of the quilting community: quilters never go quilting without *Jack the Ripper*!

6

LET THE SEWING BEGIN

Seated in the lounge already, Celia, Charlotte, and Betty looked eager to begin. Alex scanned the room, but Joey was not present. She would not be upset with him if he hung out with Arthur instead. She couldn't blame him for his youth.

Besides the Spruce Street pack, Alex counted six other women and one man. Alex found the seat with the place card with her name. She was next to Birdie, Arthur's mom, who was —dare she say it—*drunk*. Again? Still?

Celia introduced herself to everyone and made a small tribute, telling the group that this trip had been all made possible by Nona. She used Nona's given name, Gretta Galia, which gave Alex a twinge of sadness.

"I will give the floor to Jane, who is going to give us a quick lesson about the storm at sea quilt that we will be working on." Celia said.

Like yesterday, Jane was not doing a very good job hiding whatever was going on with her. She was fidgety and kept glancing at the door.

"As Celia stated, we will be working on a storm at sea quilt over the next week. The kits have been provided, and you will find all the essentials at your sewing station. The machines have been generously provided by Sewlock, a US-based sewing machine company. If anyone needs a quick lesson on how to operate these sewing machines, I will be glad to assist."

Alex speculated about what might be going on with the woman, which was really none of her business. *Does she not want to teach the quilters? That doesn't seem likely.*

Jane unfolded a gorgeous tropical quilt. "This is a storm at sea quilt. It is an optical illusion. Though it looks like a pattern of curves, every seam is actually straight, and if you plan it just right, you will have plenty of time to work on it." She then pointed to the kit on her table. "Inside the kit, you will find the pattern and your fabric. All the pieces have been pre-cut for you, so we can get right to work on sewing. Raise your hand if you are unfamiliar with the Quilt'N'Sew sewing machine. I will come around and help get you started." Jane raised her own hand and eyed the group for anyone needing assistance.

Alex surveyed the seating arrangement as she sat between Charlotte and Birdie and in front of Betty. She wished she had been seated *behind* Betty. Celia was sandwiched between two other passengers Alex had yet to meet, both with their hands raised.

"Why don't we go around and introduce ourselves to each other while I give Betty and Paul a quick demo on their machines?" Jane asked as she crossed the room to assist them.

Betty doesn't need help with a sewing machine. What is she up to?

As a defense attorney, Alex was no stranger to speaking in front of people and introducing herself. Though she often got a twinge of nerves for no apparent reason, like it was the first day of law school all over again. *It's got to be the suit,* she thought and chuckled. *An expensive suit can make the difference as to*

*whether you feel confident or not, but things just haven't been the
same since . . . Nona's death.*

Of course, Betty spoke up first. "My name is Betty Reckorc,
and I am from Spruce Street."

Charlotte scoffed and turned, giving her a look.

Betty continued. "Salem, Massachusetts, that is."

Geez, this *was* a bit like high school. Alex smirked. Not that
this was the time for any deep reflection, but she really had to
work harder on her disciplined countenance or let it go all
together. Since arriving back on Spruce Street four months ago,
her cool exterior had been tested, her inner strength weakened,
and her resolve was nowhere to be found. Once it was gone,
there was no telling what her facial features would reveal at any
given moment! She was like her father in that she could make a
dozen different expressions per second.

Alex was deep in her own thoughts. She barely heard Charlotte introduce herself. Then, she realized all eyes were on her.
"Oh, sorry. I am Alex, also from Salem, Mass."

As the attendees went around the room introducing themselves, she lost her focus again and barely caught Arthur's mom
saying something about Australia and that she was a stay-at-
home parent from Sheboygan on this cruise with her family.

"Okay," Jane said. "All the machines have been pre-
threaded with a gorgeous aqua one-hundred-percent-cotton
thread from the MagniThread company. You will find extra
thread and pre-wound bobbins in your kit. You're welcome to
take everything home with you at the end. Except for the
machines, of course. However, they are available for purchase."

The women began rifling through their quilt kits and
admiring the threads.

Jane continued, "You have each been provided a set of tools
to use during the cruise. Those are yours to keep and take home
with you."

She raised a small clear plastic tote full of sewing notions. Alex heard the simultaneous unzipping of all the little cases as they began to investigate the goodies provided.

Jane held up each of the tools as she resumed, "Each of you should have one rotary cutter, the number one staple of every quilter's tool kit. Please remember, safety *on,* every time you set the cutter down." She flicked the safety slide up and down several times to reiterate and then set the shiny cutter on the table. "You shouldn't need to use it much, but it comes with a platinum blade that will last!"

Betty mumbled something incoherent, no doubt a quiet rebuke for the use of the tool in the spirit of her best friend, Nona, who hadn't approved of the use of rotary cutters, never having used one in her life.

"You will also find a box of pins, a seam ripper, and a stiletto. Not the stabby kind. If you are not familiar with a stiletto, you will use this as an extra finger to assist you with accurate piecing," she said, showing the quilting notions. "Also, a small six-and-a-half-inch ruler and a small pair of fabric scissors." Next, Jane displayed a small Ziploc bag filled with colorful plastic pieces. "These are pinnable block markers. You can slide your pin through the hole at the top and use the alpha or numerical markers to keep track of the pieces within the block." Jane packed her set of tools back into her clear plastic case. "The kit is laser cut, and you can see each pile is a set of the different pieces that make up the block." Jane presented the plastic box containing the stacks of precut fabric pieces snuggled into the box. "Today, we are going to make one block together. The room will be set up going forward for your use every day between breakfast and lunch and after dinner until midnight. I will be available for help during the morning hours should you need anything."

The evening time slot was perfect for Alex. She had always

been a bit of a night owl. Though, she pondered if she could get it done in just the evening hours alone, plus the two they were currently working in. She might as well try to do both sets of hours whenever she could. *Not every day, though,* she promised herself. As much as she wanted to bury herself in a quilting project, she also wanted to take advantage of the calming waters surrounding them.

Alex was a fast and meticulous sewer, but she knew from past classes, it would likely take nearly this entire session to get through the first block. Though she had never made a storm at sea quilt before, it was, at most, intermediate-level work. This was one of her bucket list quilts to make, along with a log cabin and her own grandmother's flower garden quilt, of course.

The sample quilt Jane had shown was stunning. Overly excited to make the quilt, she unlatched the plastic case to pat the fabrics—luxurious quilting cottons from Harmony Fabrics. She opened the pattern and sat contentedly in her own little world as she read through the instructions.

When she was nearly finished reading through the whole pattern, Charlotte broke through her concentration. "Alex, are you up for the late-night hours?"

"Yes, for sure." Alex nodded eagerly.

"Let the biddies have the daytime hours." Charlotte grinned.

"I think I am going to try to do both, as much as possible, to make sure I can get the quilt top done. I do not need another WIP," she replied to Charlotte.

The *biddies* and the *youngins* were a friendly inside joke in the neighborhood, though it always sounded like they were a West Side quilt gang when she thought of it that way. Charlotte was lovingly, if not a little snarkily, describing how the quilters in the two age brackets referred to each other back in Salem. The older quilters who had previously met with Nona at number 1 were the biddies. The younger quilters, fifty and under, that met at the Nuts & Bolts Quilt Shop on Main Street back home, were the youngins. Neither group took offense to the slang, though keeping them separate had been mostly Nona's doing. Alex, with the help of Sue, the quilt shop owner, had been on a secret mission to merge the two groups. The two age brackets had a lot to learn from one another.

Alex looked around at the other guests and guessed Charlotte was referring to Betty, as she was the only octogenarian in the room save for the man, Paul. Betty could be a little much when it came to her meddling and gossip, though it did come in handy sometimes. Alex had to keep reminding herself that Betty had lost her best friend, her partner in crime, when Nona had been murdered. Maybe she would get along with the male quilter, and he could keep Betty the Busybody busy! *Ha, that was cute.*

At the front of the room, Jane said, "Take one piece from each of the stacks. Keep them in order. If you need to, you can label the piles and pieces with the pins provided. Just stick a pin in each pile so you remember which is which. Once we have completed the first block and you understand the construction of it, you can chain-piece the rest. I will teach you the chain-piecing method where you make each step of the process for all of the blocks in the quilt top, without breaking thread and before moving on to the next step, like an assembly line. I will show you before the end of the class."

Alex removed one piece from each stack and placed them in order on her table to the right of her machine. They had been given block-sized wool pressing mats and seam rollers in place of irons. There was a single ironing station with a cordless Orlisimo iron set up at the back of the room for all to use as needed.

Having been under Nona's tutelage and all accomplished

quilters, the women from Spruce Street didn't really need a class per se, but like most quilters, they all enjoyed classes for the chance to spend time together.

Alex pieced the block together in the order Jane had instructed. She referred to the diagram on the pattern just to make sure she had it right before sewing. It was good practice to read through the pattern, as she had, and understand the pattern designer's method rather than making assumptions about how one *thought* they should do it. Making assumptions or missing key steps often got quilters tripped up. Whenever Alex took classes at the local quilt shop, Sue emphasized this every chance she got. Not only was Sue a good saleswoman, she was a fabulous teacher with an excellent understanding of the quilting craft. What Alex hadn't learned from Nona, she'd learned from Sue over the years.

In New York, Alex had occasionally met up at a crafting spot where all were welcome to come and work on anything from stamping to sewing. It was not a convenient location, and it had been tough to work around her hours at the law firm. Not to mention that she'd had to drag around her twenty-eight-pound sewing machine, which she lovingly referred to as Hercules.

Just as Alex had expected, after only one quick break for a snack, the quilting time was nearly up already, and most of the quilters had just about finished their first block. It always amazed Alex that they could get so swept up in quilting that the time just flew by, drowning out everything in the world yet leaving her with the feeling that there was never enough time.

"Okay, I think everyone's completed the first block." Jane stood with her back to Birdie. "Let's hold up the blocks for everyone to see."

Alex could see the frustration mounting on Birdie's face as she didn't have her block done. Unmoving, Jane looked around to see all the quilters proudly holding up their blocks in front of her. They were identical because of the precut kits provided. However, the scrappy nature of fabrics caused the block design to stand out more on some than others. Depending on how each person laid out the fabrics, each person in the group could conceivably have an ever so slightly different quilt.

Alex picked up a pile and shuffled the pieces, repeating with each pile to ensure her quilt would be unlike any of the others.

After class ended, there was just about an hour of free time before dinner. The short, seven-night cruise was due to arrive at its island destination, still unknown to Alex, within three-days' time.

Alex said to Celia, "I am going to check on Joey and Arthur and then lounge on the deck with my book . . . or maybe better yet, I think I will get in a quick siesta." Saying it aloud, Alex was instantly transported back to Spruce Street. Although Nona was not of Spanish or Latin descent, she had always referred to her nap time as a siesta.

Charlotte and Birdie stood huddled near the door, chatting. Alex could smell the alcohol in the air as she made her way by. She wasn't a heavy drinker herself and had no issues with others indulging.

Birdie said, "I am sure the guys are fine. Arthur is a very responsible young man. He takes after his old man."

Heading to Joey's cabin, Alex thought about Arthur and his parents and had a hard time believing that his dad wouldn't want him on the trip, unless it was supposed to be just for Ernesto and Birdie. Alex assumed Arthur was Ernesto's biological son, based on what Birdie had said, although they bore no resemblance to each other. The father was a well-fed, stout man —a caricature straight from a scene in an old mafia movie— while the son was thin and gangly. When she had seen him last, Arthur had been wearing board shorts, tennis shoes, and a horizontally striped shirt that looked like it had time-warped from the eighties movie, *Stand By Me*, even though the kid was around twenty.

Thinking about Arthur reminded Alex of the promise she'd made to Joey's parents, that she would keep an eye on him. With no children of her own, she was feeling a little maternal about her job to watch over him, though he was a grown young man.

Alex knocked on the door to Joey's cabin, but he didn't answer.

Birdie passed Alex in the hallway and stopped at the door just past Joey's. The two boys had single cabins next to one another on the right-hand side of the hall where the single cabins were located. She looked up at Birdie and smiled but didn't make conversation. *If she's lucky, she will pass right out!*

Alex looked on as Jane passed by hurriedly. *There's that scowl again. She sure isn't happy today.*

Joey and Alex had agreed to use their cell phones if needed. Though they had no calling functions this far out on the ocean, they had tested the text messaging to make sure it would work. It did.

Knocking a second time, she shrugged. There was no reason to be alarmed that he hadn't answered the door. She wanted him to be out and about on the ship, enjoying himself. Joey was a capable young adult and didn't need Alex to helicopter-parent him during the cruise... but she still felt the urge to check in with him just the same. She would send him a text.

A few doors down at her own cabin, Alex placed the key card over the door, and the lock chimed as she entered. The room was different, smothering hot. She checked the thermostat, wondering if it was broken, only to see that it was still set at 68. Nothing seemed out of place around the room, but she could have sworn the balcony door had been shut when she had left earlier. She walked to the other side of the suite and closed the slider. It didn't make sense to have the air conditioning running with the door open. That was just wasteful.

It was evident that housekeeping had been in. The bed had been made, and there was a new towel origami, a huge swan. Alex wanted to sit with it and figure out how they had made it, but the catnap won out. She sat on the edge of the bed and slipped off her tennis shoes.

Something didn't seem right and was nagging at her, but Alex gave in, knowing the answers would come. She lay back diagonally across the bed—so as to not disrupt the swan—onto the layers of soft pillows and closed her eyes, wondering if she was missing something. *Is it just an air of paranoia or nothing in particular?*

Alex woke a short time later, just in time for the start of the dinner service. She had dreamed vividly about her childhood, her loving parents, and then moments from her teenage years with Nona, including Nona dressed as a ninja and then like an old-fashioned spy with a spyglass and a treasure map. *Must be the ship.*

Dinner was very pleasant, held on the private outdoor deck again. Most of the Spruce Street group was in attendance, including Joey, who gave her a play-by-play of everything he and Arthur had done during the day. The two young men had managed to find plenty to keep them occupied, from card games to seabird watching. Alex wasn't keen on Arthur teaching Joey how to play blackjack or poker, though.

"Have you been smoking, Joey? You stink like cigar smoke."

"Well, Arthur and I were hanging out by the yacht club. Maybe we picked it up over there?" he suggested shyly.

Alex shrugged it off. *Guys will be guys.*

The tables were lit with a golden glow from the twinkle lights overhead and the unique orange-quilted glass candle holders on each table. The smell of the grill was mouthwatering combined with the salty air. All of the dishes presented to them were irresistible choices. Joey opted for a gourmet cheeseburger and garlic truffle fries. He had actually said, "Hold the gourmet" to the waiter, which made everyone at the table laugh. Joey's face reddened.

Alex decided on a dish with beautifully grilled lamb chops, baby potatoes, and carrots seasoned with herbs and just one cocktail. Like the quilt they were working on, the drink was called *Storm at Sea*. Though she had no idea what the individual alcohols were, the cocktail, combined with a single large ice cube, made for the most delicious after-dinner drink. She was mostly intrigued by the description in the menu, which listed the glass as having been *smoked with cinnamon*, offering a hint of spice to the drink. She knew she could only have one if she wanted to actually make it to the quilting session. Other quilters could sew just fine while drinking. She could not.

Dinner was followed by a sampling of delicate desserts. Waiters set down small white plates in front of the dinner guests. Each plate had four single-bite desserts—a decadent mini cheesecake; a cupcake with a sliver of chocolate delicately placed atop the frosting; a miniature donut drizzled with caramel, no bigger than the top of a spool of thread; and Alex's favorite, a chocolate-covered strawberry, large and super sweet with a swirl of dark-and-white chocolate coating.

Fresh from her earlier nap, rejuvenated by the delicious meal, and jazzed up by the sweet desserts, Alex took her seat in the quilting room, ready to get some serious sewing done. The room was split by an enormous divider that cut the room in half, separating the quilting area from the dining side. The quilting area was closed off during meal times and opened again for the quilting sessions.

Alex chain-pieced the first of the three major steps in

constructing the blocks. She sewed in her own little universe, not paying very much attention to the others in the room, only catching bits of conversations during the moments she took her foot off the pedal. She could hear Betty giggling and Paul chuckling. It did seem they were getting along, and Alex was thrilled that Betty had found a companion for the trip.

Deciding to take a quick break for a drink, Alex scanned the room. Neither Lucy nor Arthur's mom, Birdie, was in attendance, and she assumed they were with their husbands. Alex sipped from her water bottle.

"Did you hear about Birdie?" Betty said to Alex's right.

Startled, Alex choked on her water. Coughing, she managed to get out, "No, Betty, but I suspect you are about to tell me."

"Oh, I just heard that she caused a scene today."

"And . . ." Alex prompted.

"Nothing. That's it," Betty said ruefully and walked away.

Alex stared after her. *The gossip must be terrible today if that's all she has.*

7

DAY TWO

Alex woke in the morning, groggy. The day before had been a long day, even though she had had a siesta before dinner. The quilting until midnight had taken its toll. Maybe she wasn't as young as she felt anymore.

She shook off the sleep and set out clothes to wear for the day. The water pressure in the shower was good, and the warm water was soothing, though it didn't do much to wake her up. The luxurious bath accoutrements made the shower that much more sensational.

By the time she had dried off and dressed, it was just before 7 a.m. She checked the concierge book for the day's itinerary, which called for breakfast in the private lounge, followed by free time—which she would spend quilting—until they would all be expected to meet up again on deck 8 for another mingles event for lunch. Alex had initially thought Celia was behind the events, but she knew better. Nona had planned this trip to a T. The group of Spruce Street residents lived in their own little world-bubble, and this was Nona's way of expanding them beyond that.

When Alex arrived at the lounge at the end of the hall, no one was there yet. This morning, she made herself a small plate of fruit and added a small corn muffin. No hot chocolate, no heavy breads, or protein. Her stomach was still full from the last meal, so she opted for fruit juice and a bottle of water and made her way to the outer deck. She was watching a seabird dive for its morning breakfast when Charlotte pulled up a seat next to her with a similarly small plate of food.

"Dinner was amazing last night," Charlotte said.

Alex nodded in appreciation.

"This is wonderful, Alex. Despite everything that has happened, I think we all needed this trip . . . and the quilting time, of course," Charlotte said with a contented look in her eyes.

"I have to admit I have been out of sorts and just not myself at all since Nona passed, and I have no shortage of trepidation about cruising, but it is nice to be out here on the water. It is so peaceful and relaxing." Alex cast her gaze toward the vast expanse of deep blue ocean water surrounding them and smiled at the seabird swooping past again. "And of course, the quilting is just what we needed."

"I wonder where we are going?" Charlotte cocked an eyebrow at Alex.

"Your guess is as good as mine. Most likely somewhere in the Caribbean," Alex suggested.

"Yeah, you're probably right, but there are so many islands between the Atlantic Ocean and the Caribbean Sea." They sat there staring off into the horizon. "I overheard Pete telling Lucy that he was hoping our destination was the Turks and Caicos Islands, but I secretly hope we are going to Jamaica." Charlotte's eyes beamed bright with excitement.

"Well, it's only the start of the second full day aboard, with only one more to go until we arrive. We'll know soon enough. I think I might like to find out that we are going to Costa Rica," Alex said lazily, "but I don't think we're going that far in just three days there and three days back. Most likely headed for somewhere in the Bahamas."

"I have never really been on vacation, you know," Charlotte said absently.

"Me either. It's been all work and no play for me. It's nice to finally relax," Alex said, but she couldn't help thinking this was the calm before the storm.

They sat together picking at their breakfast and watching the gentle waves in the vast expanse of water.

"Anywhere we go is fine by me," Charlotte replied a few minutes later.

After breakfast, Alex skipped the morning quilting session in favor of spending the time outside and wandering the ship.

On her way back to deck 8 for the mingles lunch, Alex bumped into Arthur's dad, Ernesto, on deck 5. He was a curious man with an interesting style of wardrobe. This time, he wore a white Panama hat with a black silk band to accompany his shorts and buttoned-down collared shirt.

"The young men are getting along smokingly," he said casually.

Alex instinctively crossed her arms. *That is an odd turn of phrase. Maybe he is trying to be coy, or it is something from his culture or a subtle hint that the boys have really been smoking.*

"Yes, Joey told me all about it over dinner last night. I hope they don't run out of things to do," she replied earnestly, wondering if there really was enough on board for two twenty-year-old boys.

"Oh, guys will be guys. They'll find something to keep them occupied," he said with a mischievous smile. "Maybe they'll find a pair of young ladies to hang out with."

The look on his face, what she'd first interpreted as mischief, went deeper. Something else was lurking behind his grin.

"Sure. Well, I am headed to the luncheon. Gotta run," Alex said.

She abruptly turned to walk in the opposite direction before he could protest. It wasn't the way she needed to go in, but she didn't care. She could take an elevator, the stairs, or loop around, anything to avoid Ernesto. Her gut intuition had never let her down before, and for a reason she didn't know, her gut told her to get going.

Looping around the deck one more time, she didn't see Ernesto again, so she made her way to the yacht club. It certainly wasn't the kind of club she would attend back home, despite her wealth, but it was clearly part of Nona's plan to get her to *mingle* there.

Rather than sitting with the Spruce Street neighbors, she opted for a table off to the side, opposite where Ernesto now sat with his wife, Birdie. In a bold move, almost an act of defiance, she randomly sat down across from a man giving off a much different vibe. He was relaxed, a gentler-looking man who Alex would've labeled a silver fox. Truth be told, she had a thing for slightly older men. Though still single, she counted herself lucky that she was not attracted to the bad boys like Charlotte was. This delicacy of a man was classic in every way.

Sadly, he reminded her of Hawk, the private investigator Alex had utilized on cases at her old law firm. Over the last few months, Hawk had gone from co-worker to dear friend to what? What was he to her now? Protector? That seemed antiquated. Even though he was in his early fifties, he was a bit old-fashioned, like Humphrey Bogart in Casablanca. All Alex needed was her own jumper dress, and she could be his Ingrid Bergman.

Would she describe him as her confidant? He surely was that, now that Nona wasn't there to be her number one. She had found herself calling on Hawk for more than just conversation about the case. He wasn't her lover, yet, though they had come close to kissing, once, while working on Nona's murder case. Alex was vulnerable, and the temptation had been there on several occasions as they had worked late into the night at her home on Spruce Street, but Hawk had never acted on it.

Alex knew the feelings were mutual. She was sure of that. For her, the constant flutter in her stomach every time she was around him was proof enough.

"Hi, I'm Alex," she said, holding out her hand to shake the silver fox's.

Leaning forward, he raised his hand to *take* hers, not shake it. He held it for a moment, and she could smell his aftershave— earthy, like fall in New England after the leaves had dropped and the rain had passed. He wore an unbuttoned linen shirt over a mélange T-shirt. This gentleman looked to be in his mid- to late-fifties, tan and well-toned for his age.

Letting go of her hand, he said, "Pleased to meet you. My name is Jon Draper."

She smiled and held back a chuckle, thinking of the character in the television series *Mad Men*. He didn't resemble the famous actor who played Don Draper, not physically anyway.

The two struck up an easy conversation, and she quickly learned the man's cabin was in the same corridor as hers, just on the opposite side of the elevator bank. He chatted with her about how he'd found himself to be on this cruise, and she explained how Nona had set this up for all the residents in her neighborhood. He opened up about his late wife and how they used to cruise together every year. She assumed it was recent as he still bore a tan line where his ring would have been.

Alex kept up her end of the conversation, sharing about her life in New York City before coming home to Salem, Massachusetts. She learned he'd retired from the military and was dabbling in the culinary field. They sat companionably staring into the deep blue ocean. A gentle, warm breeze blew against the side of her neck while the man regaled her with tale after tale. Alex began to warm to him. Stories of travel, culture, and a growing list of impressive restaurants intrigued her. She really did enjoy the company, even though deep down she was still wishing she had taken Hawk up on his offer to come along on the cruise. Of course, she didn't need his protection, and there was no case to work, but it was obvious to her that this was what she needed in her life—companionship.

Alex saw Joey and Arthur across the deck, eating, picking at their food like birds.

He's way too skinny. She found herself trying, mostly in vain, to feed him every time he visited her on Spruce Street. That thought made her realize it was about time she checked in on Spruce Street—Alastor and Kibbles, to be exact.

"This has been very enjoyable, but it is time I excuse myself. I have to call home to check on the sitter," she said.

Mr. Draper stood. "The pleasure is all mine, Alex. I hope we'll have another opportunity to *mingle* before the cruise is over," he said, emphasizing the word mingle in a way that pleased her.

"I do as well." Alex smiled and turned to go. He remained standing as she walked away.

She headed to the stern down on deck 7, where the boys swore they had the best cell reception. Leaning against the railing, she typed up a quick email to Alastor, checking in on the little pooch. Once she hit send on the email, she opened her texting app and tried sending a text message to Hawk. She was feeling just a little guilty over how much she'd enjoyed her time with Jon Draper. If the text didn't go through, she would try to video call him later, after dinner. She typed *Thinking of you* and then quickly erased it, then *Miss you*, and erased that too. Frustrated and unsure what to write, she finally decided to skip the text altogether.

She headed back to her cabin, passing Arthur's dad. Why was he always around?

The weather was hot but not muggy. There was an overhang from the deck above, so Alex was able to remain in the shade as she walked back to the stairs that led down to the Spruce Street corridor. Though the temporary signs Celia had put up had already been taken down, it had been fun to think of their neighborhood.

She looked down at her watch. It was nearly dinnertime. She had talked to Jon Draper for almost two hours.

On her way back to the stairs, she passed Jane and Ernesto standing close to one another having an animated conversation. She wouldn't have given it a second thought had Jane not been waving her hands around and pointing and poking Ernesto on the shoulder.

I can't imagine it's okay for the Windsom staff to touch a guest like that. None of your business, Alex. Keep walking. She was determined to have an uneventful, stress-free trip and not get involved in other people's affairs, unlike Betty.

After dinner, she went back to the lounge for another late night of quilting. As promised, Charlotte and Celia were not long behind her. Alex nearly finished the second step in the three-step process before she started to yawn, which caused her seam allowance to veer off. She stopped and looked for her trusty seam ripper, Jack, no more than five inches long with a seriously pointy end. *Stick 'em with the pointy end!* Alex laughed at herself, recalling the popular reference from *Game of Thrones.*

Alex poked around her table surface, prodded through the project bag, and dug around in her purse. She even lifted the machine because sometimes, seam rippers rolled underneath. For the thousandth time since becoming a quilter, she wondered why they didn't make seam rippers with one flat side. Then, she remembered that hers did have a flat side, so it probably wouldn't have rolled. Alex put her hands on her hips and scowled, frustrated that she couldn't find it anywhere. *Strange.*

She pulled out the seam ripper from the project bag provided to them and picked out the stitching on the last couple blocks. Turned out her stitching had been wavering a little longer than she'd realized. *Would someone have stolen my seam ripper? It was pricey, but you wouldn't think a quilter would steal a girl's seam ripper.*

As Alex looked around the room for the tool, she noticed she was well ahead of the class, even after she had finished restitching her seams on the three blocks. The others would have plenty of time to work on it while the Spruce Street gang was off on their mystery excursion. The time allocated on the return trip would certainly be enough for the majority of the quilters to finish their quilt tops.

Alex was disappointed that she couldn't find her tool, but her motto had always been, "It'll turn up." She was no stranger to misplacing things in her personal life. The brain capacity taken up by her job as a lawyer left little for her personal skills, and she was sometimes mindless when it came to her personal belongings. *Okay, let's face it. I am a hot mess sometimes. It's true!*

She had hoped to finish step two, but she was tired and

decided to head to bed. If she kept at it, she would just end up making mistakes.

On her way out, she noticed Betty and Paul's sewing tables had been moved side by side, and she smiled. At least things were going right for someone.

8

NOT AGAIN

After a hearty breakfast the next morning sans Joey or Arthur and then another very productive quilting session, Alex changed into a sundress and lathered herself up with sunscreen. Her skin wasn't fair but she hadn't spent any significant time in the sun in a few years. She grabbed the book she'd brought—*Beach Brawl: A Quilting Cozy Mystery* by her favorite author, Kate Michaels—and headed to the elevator.

Alex stepped off the elevator onto deck 7, where it was noticeably hotter than it had been at breakfast on the private deck off the lounge. She walked three quarters of the way around the deck without a Joey sighting then made her way to the deck chairs. The natural shade from the deck above had apparently gone off duty. The sun beamed right down on her. Grateful for sunscreen, she stopped at a string of empty seats.

Luckily, the crowd meandered to the poolside bar on the opposite side of the ship. Alex had the area to herself, a nice, quiet, peaceful place to read her book. She chose the chair at the far end, facing the rest of the open deck, a good vantage point to spot Joey if he crisscrossed the space.

Nearing the end of chapter three, Alex was just about to

find out who had died in the beach brawl when a commotion arose across the deck. She looked up and jerked. A naked man, with a familiar mop of red hair, was running straight at her, yelling incoherently and flailing wildly. Alex was just about to dive out of the way, although there really was nowhere for her to go, when his foot caught the side of the first chair. He pitched downward, hitting his head on the corner of a wooden deck chair, and belly flopped onto the deck in front of her. All flailing ceased.

Alex untangled herself from where she had landed trying to avoid the streaker. She clutched her elbow. She had hit her funny bone, and the pain emanating was anything but funny. Passengers who had seen the streaker began to run toward the scene and stopped to huddle around the naked form. As she got near, her hand shot to her mouth. It *was* Arthur, and he wasn't moving.

"Call for a medic," someone yelled.

Alex backed up the crowd so she could get in close to him. She called his name and nudged him, and finally, when there was no response, she checked his neck for a pulse, but as she had feared, she did not find one.

She was hit with an onslaught of questions from the witnesses approaching.

"What happened?"

"What was he saying?"

"Did he say 'a broom'? What does that mean?"

"Why is he naked?"

"Is he dead?"

"It's a good thing he landed facedown," a familiar voice said.

"There is nothing good about this, Pete," Alex replied in a hushed tone. "It's Arthur," she said louder, finding her full voice. "Did anyone hear what he was saying?" she asked no one in particular and everyone at the same time.

They all murmured "no" and "it makes little sense."

Jon Draper, the debonair silver fox she had spoken to the day before, spoke up to be heard over the emergency sirens. "He was incoherent. I couldn't make out what he said exactly, but it sounded like '*Help me, the pants.*'" He stepped closer to Alex as he spoke.

With the alarm blaring, the ship's security raced to the scene, and the ship's doctor was not long behind them. He bent to check for a pulse, and he confirmed Arthur was, in fact, deceased. The doctor made a brief call, and minutes later, two medical attendants came and covered Arthur's body with a white sheet and carefully lifted him onto a gurney.

"His mother?" Alex questioned. "Someone needs to get his parents."

"We will," the attendant said. "We're going to need to speak with each of you who saw the young man just prior to his untimely death."

"He was running toward her," one of the onlookers said and pointed at Alex.

"Why don't you come with us, Miss—?"

"Bailey. Alex Bailey," she responded to the doctor's question.

"Miss Bailey, you can give the ship's head of security an account of what happened," he said as he motioned for her to follow.

In just a turn of the page, she had gone from calm sun-basking glory to a tragic death of a young man, and she still didn't know who the beach brawl killer was.

"Yes, I am happy to tell you what I know." She frowned. "Which isn't much. Let me change first, and I will meet you."

She wasn't going to be interrogated in a sundress. *I am still a lawyer*, she reminded herself. She had the sense to know she needed slacks and a sensible blouse at least.

"Sure, sure." He nodded while simultaneously giving her an inappropriate appraisal, a once-over from head to toe.

All the more reason to change.

"Come to the medical suite on deck 3," he said and eyed one of the security personnel.

"This way, miss. I will escort you," he said.

As she reached her suite, chaperone in tow, she mindlessly fumbled with the key card. Entering her room, she tossed her book onto the bed. She rinsed off her arms and legs with a wet hand towel and splashed some water on her face. After changing into a sensible outfit—slacks and a casual cotton top—she coiled her hair in a tight bun, which pulled all the hair off her face and neck and made her look as serious as she could manage, given she was on a vacation cruise.

Alex followed the security officer to the medical facility on deck 3. The small area was filled with only two hospital beds, a couple portable first aid stations, and three staff—one doctor, one nurse, and an aide. She shook hands with the doctor and reminded him again of who she was.

"What did you find? Did he die from the fall on the deck?" Alex began her familiar interrogation tack.

The doctor shook his head, and just as he was about to utter an answer, Arthur's mom, Birdie, came barging in. She screamed at Alex, shaking her finger.

"What did you do to my son? It's all your fault!" She stood just a foot away, close enough that Alex could feel Birdie's breath.

My fault? Why? How could it be my fault? I did nothing.

Arthur's dad, Ernesto, stood formidably across most of the doorway and was no longer displaying the behavior of a jolly . . .

or creepy . . . Joe. A vein pulsed on his forehead, and it was setting off Alex's flight response.

Birdie turned between Alex and Ernesto and repeated her accusing question. "What have you done to my son?"

Ernesto's nostrils flared.

Wait, which of us is she asking? And why would Birdie be accusing either of us? It doesn't make sense.

"I have done nothing to your son. I was just a witness." Alex stepped backward from the wave of fury emanating from the pair, like heat waves on blacktop.

Alex put her hands up in defense and continued backing her way toward the doctor. With the doctor's helpful persuasion, the group shifted in a clockwise dance, moving Ernesto out of the door and leaving Alex closer to an escape.

"Look, I can see you are upset," Alex said. "I am sorry for your loss. I am going to go."

Alex made eye contact with the doctor, who gave her an apologetic nod.

She gave him a look that said *Good luck, Doc,* and exited the medical suite in a hurry.

"You will pay," Birdie shrilled behind her.

She's clearly blaming me, but for what? Being a witness?

Alex's phone chirped and startled her, causing her to jump. She lifted the phone from her back pocket. It was a text message. A picture of Hawk's loafers and a drink with a fancy umbrella with the caption "Jealous?" made her chuckle.

"What?" Birdies shriek echoed down the corridor.

Alex shoved her phone back in her pocket. Desperate to get out of the corridor and into the safety of the open air, she pushed open the door so hard she nearly knocked over an elderly couple.

"I am so sorry," she apologized profusely.

The husband grabbed the wife's arm and ushered her

quickly through the door, mumbling, "Watch where you're going."

Alex rushed to the railing and nearly slipped on a giant bird dropping, narrowly catching the railing and keeping herself upright. *The grace of a hooked fish, Alexandra,* she could hear her mom say in the back of her mind, from when she was young.

She held the railing for stability, headed for the closest deck chair, and tucked herself gently into it. All she needed now was a quilt. Alex pulled her hair out of the bun and scratched her scalp where the hair had been pulling. With a quick shake of her head, her hair fell naturally to her shoulders.

Poor Joey, what a crazy day.

After seeing Hawk's lounge chair snapshot, she was thinking maybe she should have gone *with Hawk* on his adventure rather than wishing *he* had joined *her* on this trip. Well, it was too late now.

She settled more comfortably into the chair trying not to dwell on Arthur's unfortunate accident.

9

NO SUCH THING AS A COINCIDENCE

WITHOUT A QUILT TO SNUGGLE IN, SHE STARED UP AT THE setting sun and let the afternoon heat comfort her. This was all just coincidence, she hoped, but was it? Another dead person? She knew in her gut there was no such thing as coincidence.

Another quick shake of her head removed the thoughts of hit men and murder that had invaded her mind upon seeing another deceased person. Alex wrapped her arms around herself. She had *thought* she was safe aboard the *Tranquility*, but she was *feeling* anything but safe right now. When her heart had finally slowed to a normal rhythm, she convinced herself that she was going to be fine.

In the weeks leading up to the departure, Hawk and his hacker friend, Miss White, had combed through the passenger manifest and vetted the staff members. The only way he was willing to let Alex aboard without him was if he had found no connection to her old law firm, Weitz & Romano, to New York and even to Las Vegas, where Nona's murderer had been from. Obviously, some people would probably have connections up north, but she was as safe as anyone else on board. Hawk had made sure she wasn't going to unexpectedly find herself at sea with a hit man.

Arthur's death is none of your business, Alex thought. *Answer the questions, report on only what you saw, and stay out of it!* She was reciting the mantra in her mind when Joey skidded up to her chair.

"Watch ou—" she began.

He narrowly missed slipping on the *pile,* as Alex had done minutes ago.

He looked back. "Geez, that's the biggest pile of . . . bird. . .?" His eyes scrunched as he tried to get a better look. "Biggest pile of crap I've ever seen!"

She laughed at his assessment. He wasn't wrong.

"I hope it is 'bird's'!" she replied, and they both snickered. "Why are you in such a hurry?"

"I wanted to ask you. Could you help figure out what happened to Arthur?" The youthful concern on his face made her heart melt. "He was my friend, and I know you can help."

"Gosh, Joey, I am sorry. I wasn't thinking," she said, and without hesitation, she hugged him. Cupping his shoulders with her hands and putting him at arm's length, she asked, "What do you mean help? Help with what?"

"Can you find out why?" he replied with pleading eyes.

"What do you mean why? I saw him fall on the deck, and..." She gulped. "He died." She lowered her head in remorse. "It is up to the ship's medical staff and security to handle it now."

"I was with him yesterday, and everything was fine." Joey choked up. "He didn't show up last night. We were supposed to meet at . . ." He trailed off.

Alex gave one more gentle squeeze of his shoulders and let go of him. "I'm not sure we should get involved, Joey. His parents are really upset. I think we need to give his family some space to let them grieve. Besides, I am a lawyer, not a doctor. I have no medical training," she reminded him.

"But we were to meet at his parents' cabin and—"

Alex cut him off. "What were you going to do at his parents' cabin? I thought he had his own cabin next to yours." Her tone was sharp.

Joey winced. He bent his head and chewed on his lip for a couple seconds. "Well, okay, we were there to sneak another cigar from his father's private stash," he blurted. "Arthur said his father purchased only the finest cigars. Cuban and very expensive."

Alex shook her head. *Guys will be guys.* She was reminded of her own thoughts as well as Ernesto's words. He probably would have given the boys the cigars himself.

"Okay, so beyond a little mischief, I'm sure your parents taught you not to steal," she chided, and his face turned a shade similar to that of a ripe red apple. "How does this apply to Arthur's death?" she added, letting him off the hook for the moment.

"I don't know," he said, his tone defeated. "We had a plan to meet and get the cigar . . . and we planned to smoke it up on deck 8 like the rich people do. He didn't show, so I looked around for a while and then went to bed. Alex, you have to believe me," he pleaded.

"Okay, settle down. Of course I believe you. Look, let's give the ship's staff and his family some time to process what's happened. In the meantime, I don't want you to talk to anyone about Arthur unless I am present," she said firmly. "I am serious, Joey. Do not talk to anyone!"

"Like you will be my legal counsel?" he asked shyly. "Do you think I need it?"

"No, no, nothing like that." She patted his hand. "But stay away from his father . . . both of his parents," she added. "They are both a bit . . . scary . . . right now. They're upset, and I don't want them taking it out on you unnecessarily."

Like they did to me.

Alex mustered the most reassuring smile she could. "Everything will be all right." Then, her maternal instinct kicked in. "How about we go get some lunch?"

"Okay," he said, standing up. "I guess I could eat."

"Food always makes me feel better." She smiled encouragingly and led him toward the snack bar.

Joey walked ahead of Alex with his shoulders slumped.

Poor thing. We'll have to find something for him to do now, to take his mind off things.

He sat slouched at the table, picking at his French fries one at a time, taking a single bite then tossing it back onto his plate. Alex hadn't touched much of her salad either.

While waiting for their food, she had struck up a conversation with the crewman, who had revealed he had seen the boy running across the front of the tiki bar, and he'd thought he had heard Arthur say, "Don't."

She pushed her lettuce around with her fork, pondering what Arthur had been trying to say. *Super not helpful.* Don't? *That could mean anything!*

Alex was gazing out into the endless horizon, lost in thought, when Betty appeared behind Joey. "Alex. Joey." She nodded. "I don't know what is going on, but Jane and Celia were looking for you. They said if I saw you, to tell you to go to the brig and ask for Kane."

Betty stood with her hands on her hips with the most peculiar look, as if to say: *How is it that I don't know what is going on?*

"Do you know what's going on? There was a lot of commotion earlier. Why are they looking for you?"

"Er—" Joey started to speak, but Betty interrupted.

"Did you see anything, Joey? I was asking around . . ." She paused.

"It was my friend, Arthur. He's . . . he's dead," Joey choked out.

"Oh my." Betty put her hand over her mouth. "Not again," she said, eyeing Alex speculatively. "Oh, Alex, is the ship safe? You assured us . . ."

"You're in no danger, Betty. I'm sure this has nothing to do with me, or us, or Spruce Street. It was just an unfortunate accident." Alex waved her off and glared at Joey. *I told you not to say anything to anyone.*

"A coincidence, you think?" Betty asked and then answered her own question. "No, there are no such things as coincidences in a mystery. You must know that."

"I don't know, Betty. Who claimed this was a mystery?" Alex's tone was sharper than she had intended. "The young man tripped and fell. Anything more than that, I do not know."

"Well, I spoke to a few passengers on the way over here, and one of them said he saw Arthur run by yelling. He said Arthur kept repeating the same thing, but he didn't know what he was trying to say. He thought he was saying, 'Warn you,'" Betty said.

Warn you? Well, another not-so-helpful tidbit. Warn who and about what? Was Arthur purposefully running toward me? To warn me? But about what?

"Help me," "the pants," "don't," and now, "warn you."

She frowned. Something was definitely not right about this whole thing.

Betty was still jabbering on, but Alex had drowned out her voice with her thoughts. *How can Betty possibly think this young man's tragic death has anything to do with Spruce Street or me?*

"If we hadn't been . . ." Joey began to mumble.

Alex cut him off with another warning look. The last thing

she wanted was for Betty to get any ideas that Joey was involved.

Alex looked at Joey's half-eaten meal. "I don't think either of us is going to eat. Why don't we head to the lounge to relax for a little while?" She stood and motioned for Joey to stand as well. "Betty," Alex said and nodded goodbye.

Alex quickly ushered Joey away. The last thing Alex needed was Betty meddling or dragging Alex and Joey into it any further. If there was anything to the young man's death, she wanted to get information *from* Betty, not give.

"I don't think you should talk to Betty about any of this," Alex said out of earshot just in case her pointed looks hadn't made her point.

They continued the conversation, circling the deck to the door that led to the steps.

"Joey, I think you should explain to me everything that you remember . . . while it's still fresh in your mind. *Before* I go meet this Kane guy."

"Okay, well, I went to meet Arthur to get the cigar, but he wasn't there. I have no idea where he went. I wandered around for a while then went to bed. I figured I would see him in the morning, but he didn't show up to our breakfast spot, so I went looking for him again. That was when I heard the commotion on the deck . . . and you know the rest."

Alex opened the door to the stairwell.

Joey stopped next to her and said, "Maybe he slipped on that pile of bird doo?"

"Maybe," Alex said half-heartedly.

"His parents can't go home thinking he died because he slipped on a bird turd."

"How did you get in before? To the cabin, I mean?"

"Arthur had a key card. Technically, we did nothing wrong," Joey said with an innocent look.

"Well, that's not *really* true," she said, following him down the stairs.

Joey stopped mid-step and turned to Alex, his deep blue eyes pleading for reassurance.

"I *really* don't want you to get involved, Joey. Heck, *I* really don't want to get involved either," Alex qualified and urged him to keep going with a wave of her hand.

"My dad was a cop, Alex. It runs in my family. I can't help it! And you're a lawyer . . ."

"Not a detective," she said as they passed through the door linking the private lounge and the corridor between their cabins. "Say nothing. Leave it to me, please. I will handle it." She silenced his protest with the sternest voice she could muster.

He was such a good kid. She didn't want to be too hard on him, but thinking back to the one case she had lost in New York, she knew all too well what happened to good kids who got tangled up in something like this.

She left Joey in his cabin and went to find Kane, and they spoke at length. It turned out her concerns that Joey would be a suspect were unfounded. The head of security was a polished professional despite his hypermasculinity. After giving a full account of the situation as Joey had explained it, Kane played back some security footage of Joey's whereabouts last evening. Judging by the angle, it was a camera nearest the door to Arthur's parents' cabin. Alex watched but didn't see anything.

He paused the video and asked, "Did you hear it?" He used a small remote to rewind the video, and the video began to play again. "The cameras are not calibrated to pick up conversations, but they do catch loud noises."

Alex cocked her ear toward the bank of monitors and took a

half-step closer to the screen they were watching. She stepped back in recognition when she heard it.

"A scream," she said. It was faint, but she could hear it.

She nodded and then continued to watch. Moments later, Arthur came bounding—or crashing was more like it—out the door, hobbling on one foot and flailing his arms around. His back was turned to the camera, but they could hear more faint noises as he bumped into the walls and shrieked a few more times.

"I am surprised no one in the hall heard him," Alex said.

Kane said, "Watch."

Alex observed several people poking their heads out from their doors, but Arthur was already out of the frame by then. *Presumably in the stairwell,* Alex thought as she continued to watch the video. Joey entered the camera's frame, from the opposite direction Arthur had gone.

"You see? I believe your account of what Joey claims to have happened." He stopped the video. "We can see him waiting here for about ten minutes. He checks his watch several times. This lines up with his story about meeting Arthur. He also leaves the same way he came, the opposite of where Arthur went. I was able to find them both on various cameras, and it all tracks."

She was intrigued and concerned at the same time. What had happened to Arthur in the room?

"Was anyone in the room? When Arthur went in?" she asked.

"No. Not as far as we can tell."

"Did you search the room?" Alex asked, not sure how much he was going to share with her.

"Yes, of course. He left quite a mess. As you would expect, there was a box of cigars on the floor, and a plant had been knocked over."

Thankfully he didn't show her any footage of Arthur taking his clothes off and streaking around the boat, but she was curious enough to ask, "Why was he naked? I am not a detective or a doctor, however, it seems likely there had to be some medical . . . or psychological explanation for his actions."

"That is all I am at liberty to say at this time, Miss Bailey. We have the room cordoned off. The parents have been moved to another suite. You and Joey should steer clear of them while we investigate."

After exiting the security office, Alex was left with questions, but at least Joey was in the clear.

Why was Arthur naked when he ran toward me? What was he shouting? What was he trying to say and to whom? And how did he die right there in front of me, just by slipping and falling down on the deck? It doesn't seem likely. None of it made sense, yet.

Kane had no reason to share any professional courtesies with her, though he had, and she was grateful, so she hadn't pressed him. He hadn't asked her any more than she had offered, so if this did have something to do with Alex or Spruce Street, she certainly wasn't going to volunteer any information, especially not about the botched hit attempt on her life just months ago.

DESTINATION REVEALED

LATER THAT EVENING, THEY HAD FREE TIME FOR DINNER, so Celia and Alex grabbed the last table in the ship's bistro. Hoping for some privacy, they sat in the far corner. They soon realized they were just two tables away from Betty, Lucy, and Pete. Close enough that they overheard Betty bleating the gossip of Arthur's death to anyone who would listen.

"It looks like he slipped on a giant pile of bird sh—"

Pete interrupted Betty's gossip string. "But I heard they want to do an autopsy to find out what happened."

Pete, don't encourage her, Alex thought.

Betty asked, "They can do autopsies on the ship?"

"Makes you wonder what they are doing with the body," Pete replied. "It must be getting ripe by now."

In between bites of her dinner, Betty continued nonchalantly, "Well, I heard they put him in the freezer."

Suddenly, Alex lost her appetite completely. *Are you listening to this, Celia? Surely they didn't really do that?*

She recalled an episode of an old crime drama from television where they had emptied all of the ice cream out of the fridge to store a body on a submarine. *But they didn't really do that . . . Did they?*

"Alex?" Celia waved. "Earth to Alex."

"Oh, sorry, I was eavesdropping on Betty. What did you say?" She realized she'd been having the conversation internally and never actually asked her questions out loud to Celia.

"Nothing important." Celia smiled.

The server approached the table and took their orders.

"Betty is such a gossip, Alex. I don't know how you deal with her sometimes."

"Actually, Betty has proven to be super helpful to me since coming home to Spruce Street, though the gossip is not my style. I am thinking maybe we can direct her energy in a helpful way." Alex chuckled.

"You are not planning to get involved, are you, Alex?"

"No, no, I'm staying out of it, and I have said as much to Joey also."

"Did he have anything to do with what happened to that young man? You know, we don't really know him all that well."

"No. I spoke with security earlier, and they confirmed Joey's story. He's only been in our lives for a short time, but Nona had been getting to know him for quite some time unbeknownst to any of us."

Celia pursed her lips. "Maybe it has something to do with the kid's parents, since the guys were messing around in their cabin."

Alex had brought her up to speed on their way to dinner, so she knew everything Alex knew up to this point.

"I saw him just before . . . he, er, slipped... on the deck." Alex wasn't entirely sure what had happened. He had been flailing around and yelling things.

Celia shrugged. "It is a peculiar mystery. Something

happened in that room," she murmured as the waitress set down Celia's wine and Alex's beer. "I've heard talk of foul play, but the ship doesn't have the facilities to deal with that kind of investigation. They're suggesting it be done at our destination," Celia whispered, so as not to be overheard in the crowded restaurant.

Alex was grateful for Celia's choice of words. After all, they were about to eat dinner.

"I think it is time to tell me where we are going," Alex suggested.

"Yes, I think you are right." Celia sighed. "I am sorry."

"What are you sorry about, Celia?" Alex asked as the waiter placed their respective plates of food in front of each of the women.

"Well, first Nona, now this just months later. Seems as though death is following us." Celia shivered and made the sign of the cross. "We are headed to a marine biology center on the small island of Madras."

"Why would Nona be sending us to a marine biology center on an obscure island?"

"I really shouldn't, Alex." Celia sat back in her chair, picking at her chicken.

"It's fine. I think we're past the point where this is just a fun adventure." Alex sighed. "Tell me what you know."

"Well, actually, Nona funded the school."

Alex sat silent for a couple beats. When she realized she was going to need to coax more details from Celia, she asked, "With my money?"

Celia knew about Alex's wealth. With all of the planning to get the group on the cruise, Alex had confided in her the details as well as the arrangement she'd had with Nona. Alex and Nona had a joint account, providing Nona access to several million dollars of Alex's money.

"No, she funded the school with her own money. I think it was her retirement money. She . . ." Celia took a deep breath. "She bought the island with *your* money," she said, then stuffed a piece of broccoli in her mouth.

Alex choked on her beer, causing it to dribble on her chin. "She bought an *island*? With the money?"

While Alex wiped the beer from her chin with a napkin, Celia replied, "She told me it was the only way the school could continue. I've seen the brochure, Alex. The school has done some seriously amazing work over the last few years."

"Made possible by Nona?" Alex questioned, and Celia nodded. "Gosh, what was that woman up to? How was she able to keep so many secrets from all of us?"

Alex hung her head, saddened by the thought that she wasn't sure if she'd ever really known Nona at all.

"I don't know. She really was an enigma!"

They both laughed, and the mood instantly lifted.

"Look," Celia added, "you should also know that when we get there, some of the students are going to come aboard and give presentations and lectures to try and solicit money from all these rich passengers."

"Nona!" Alex said, shaking her head in amazement.

"It's genius, really." Celia laughed. "Cheers."

She held out her glass, but Alex wasn't sure how she felt about being a pawn in yet another of Nona's schemes. Plus, she still had Arthur's parents to contend with.

"I don't know what she was up to all those years," Alex said, "but it seems she was more than just a single mom homemaker."

"I agree with you on that point. I suspect we will be uncovering Nona's secrets for many adventures to come."

They both laughed fondly.

Alex asked, "That can't be all. What else does Nona have in store for us?"

"Well, she scheduled an island excursion for the Spruce Street bunch."

"So the students are going to entertain the passengers while we get off and do what?" Alex asked.

"Take a trip to the college building," Celia replied matter-of-factly. "Bring Henrietta . . . and those keys, too, just in case." She sipped her wine. "And now they'll be bringing the body too . . ." She trailed off.

Alex pushed her plate away. She hadn't eaten but a few bites of the pasta dish. "Arthur," she said coldly.

Finishing her wine, Celia said, "I'm concerned. I've heard whispers that the parents are really angry and think you and Joey had something to do with it."

The server approached with the fresh bottle of wine. Celia covered her wineglass with her hand, signaling that she didn't want any more, and Alex declined another beer.

"Where is Joey now?" Celia questioned.

"He's in his cabin. I told him to hang tight while we straighten this out. First, Birdie blamed me, and now, rumors that it was Joey's fault . . . I don't want this to get out of control, especially since Kane all but cleared Joey." Alex put her knife and fork down on her plate when inspiration struck. "Celia, maybe I can get into Arthur's parents' room?"

"Are you serious? That sounds dangerous! How would you even get in?" Celia leaned in as she bombarded Alex with questions. "What if the parents catch you? What you are saying is scary business."

"Shh. Not so loud."

Celia leaned back, her lips pursed, and placed her silverware on her plate, pushing it aside for the waitstaff to take.

Once the server had cleared their plates and walked away, Celia said, "Well, scary or not, I am not going to let you go alone."

"Perfect. I could use a partner in crime. I have a universal key that gets me into just about any door on the ship. Hawk didn't want to take any chances, just in case."

Celia sat forward, gaping at Alex.

Alex shot to her feet. "Are you coming?"

Celia set her napkin down and stood. "What if they're in their room?" she whispered and hurried after Alex.

Alex held out her right hand, letting Celia pass in front of her, all the while pointing with her left toward the corner of the restaurant where Birdie was sitting. Celia nodded and averted her eyes quickly. Arthur's mom sat at the table in the bar, seemingly no worse for wear but unmoving. She stared blindly at the wall with a piece of bread in one hand and her fork tucked into her pasta in the other.

"Kane said he moved them and cordoned off the room." Alex gave Celia a sly smile.

As the two women wound their way around the tables to the exit, they passed Jane on her way in. She was in her street clothes rather than her Windsom uniform.

A commotion started up behind them, and Alex glanced back. Jane and Ernesto were arguing at the other end of the bar. Just as Alex was about to leave, Jane picked up a drink from the bar, presumably Ernesto's, and threw the contents of said drink in his face. Jane stormed out past Alex. Alex moved to leave and almost bumped into Celia, who had stopped behind her, watching in shock as well.

Alex scanned the room for Birdie, but some other diners had stood up at the commotion, blocking her view.

"Quick, let's go," Alex said and urged Celia to turn around and get moving. As much as she wanted to see Birdie's reaction, Alex really didn't want to be caught standing there gawking.

When the two women were a safe distance outside the restaurant, Celia asked, "What was that all about?"

"I have no idea." Alex pushed the elevator button repeatedly, anxious to get into the elevator.

11

PARTNERS IN CRIME

They stepped off the elevator into the hallway, and something on the floor caught Alex's eye. She picked up the crumpled paper and smoothed it out, revealing a family photo.

"Birdie, Arthur, and Ernesto," Celia said.

"That's strange. Who would do this?" Alex repinned the picture to the board.

"I don't know, Alex. Maybe the parents did it in a fit of anger. You said the dad was raging."

Down the corridor, the two amateur sleuths came up to the door of Birdie's and Ernesto's cabin.

Celia nervously scanned the corridor for other passengers. She cocked her head to the side to listen. They could hear a mouse fart. It was so quiet. "Perfect timing."

Alex pressed the key card against the reader, and the door chimed to alert them it was unlocked.

Celia looked at Alex with a mischievous twinkle in her eye. "I think I like *this* kind of adventure."

"Shh." Alex put a finger to her lips as the two slipped inside the cabin and closed the door behind them.

To their surprise, the cabin was not just disturbed. It had been trashed.

"His poor parents," Celia said as she took in the scene. "What exactly are we looking for, Alex?"

"I don't know," Alex said, looking around. The cabin was identical to Alex's suite in layout.

Celia made the sign of the cross. "I can't understand how they are not out of their minds with grief right now. Look at this place." She bent over to pick something up.

"Don't touch anything," Alex whispered.

Celia stood, empty-handed. "Strange that the man would bring gloves on a tropical cruise."

Alex nodded. "I found that odd as well. I noticed that he was wearing gloves the first day. I thought maybe it was just one of his eccentricities."

"Yeah, probably. He and Birdie do seem a little . . . eccentric," Celia confirmed as she continued to scan the room. "I don't know what we are looking for, though in this mess, it's probably no use."

Alex stood in the small space dedicated to the living room. "There's the father's cigars on the floor, like Kane said." She pointed past a potted plant that had been knocked over. "Joey said they were meeting here to sneak a cigar." Alex walked toward the cigar box.

"Do you think it was the cigar that made Arthur act so strangely?" Celia asked.

"No. That's doubtful. According to Joey, the kids had already snuck one and smoked it the day before."

Alex spotted something familiar and bent to retrieve it. "Hey, this is mine." She stood, holding up a seam ripper covered in blood.

"How did that get in here?" Celia asked.

"I don't know. And why wasn't it collected as evidence?"

"I don't know. You shouldn't take it, Alex. Best to leave it where you found it. You can always get a new one."

A loud crash in the hallway caused the two women to freeze in place.

"We should probably get out of here, Alex," Celia clipped nervously.

Alex dropped the seam ripper. "Shh." She held her finger up as they stood still, listening for additional noises. Hearing none, Alex said, "I think it is safe. Let's get out of here!"

They tiptoed to the door. Alex opened it slowly, poked her head out, and scanned the hallway, but there was no one in sight. After closing the door behind them, they scurried down the hall and ducked into Alex's room a few doors down.

"That was . . . exciting." Celia wiped at her perfectly sculpted brow. "I haven't had this much fun, well, since . . . ever!"

Celia was ever the professional, never one to let her hair down, as the expression went.

Alex laughed. "Partners in crime."

"Crime *solving*," Celia retorted.

"We haven't solved anything yet! Frankly, I don't even think we are any closer to figuring this all out." Alex sat on the edge of the bed, pondering the mess that they'd seen in Arthur's parents' cabin, and then she quickly stood up again. "Do you think Birdie stole my seam ripper? On purpose? Why would she do that?"

"No one was in the room when Arthur snuck in, so he wasn't stabbed . . . Maybe Birdie's a klepto," Celia suggested.

"I think maybe we should unleash Betty and try to get some answers to what is going on around this ship."

"Are you sure about that?" Celia asked, giving Alex a perplexed look.

"As sure as I can be."

The two headed down the corridor to the group's private lounge at the end of the hall. They found Betty, but no one else was there.

"Where is everyone else?" Alex asked.

Betty shrugged, leaving Alex's question unanswered, and tucked in her blouse with the coy look of a cat that was up to no good and had been caught.

"What have you been up to, Betty?" Alex asked, ruefully.

"What have I been up to? N-Nothing. What are you asking?"

"I asked where everyone else is."

"How would I know?" Betty huffed. "It's past dinner time. They'll be here, or they won't."

Alex stood open-mouthed and wide-eyed as Betty plumped her tatas.

"Weren't you just at the bar?" Celia asked Betty.

"What if I was?"

"She *is* up to something," Celia whispered to Alex. The look on Celia's face was much the same as Alex's.

As if on cue, the staff entered the lounge and began transforming it for the towel origami class.

"I'm going to freshen up. I'll be right back," Betty said and headed for the door.

"You're not going to tell us what you've been up to?" Celia asked eagerly.

Betty flushed. "You mean who, not what." She waggled her eyebrows and strutted out of the lounge.

Since Betty had fled, giving Alex no opportunity to employ her skills of gossip and rumor collection, Alex stayed in the lounge for a towel origami session.

In the origami class, the group of strangers learned to make a simple basket, the same as the one she had seen in her room last night. A small basket holding complimentary treats—fine chocolates, a small personal-size bottle of wine, and some organic crackers—had been left the previous evening.

For their second masterpiece, they made little elephants. The instructor, Brittany, a petite young lady in her early twenties with adorable dimples and lots of freckles, giggled as she handed out googly eyes and light gray towels for each person. The elephants were for the passengers to take home as a souvenir of their trip. Brittany obviously enjoyed her job, and it was hard not to be infected by her bubbly personality, though Alex was feeling significantly older, thinking the young woman was *adorable*. She'd never before had that maternal instinct that she had been feeling as of late. Her career had kept her too busy for kids, but it had been her fears that had kept her from getting too close to any men.

After making the final towel origami—kissing swans—Alex found herself a little lighter and a little homesick . . . or was it seasick? After her pleasant conversation with Jon Draper the day before, she was still missing Hawk. Other than stubborn pride, she'd had no valid reasoning for rejecting his offer to come along on the trip.

The other passengers went on their way, and Alex found she had another brief intermission while the staff set the room back up for quilting, so she went back to her room to drop off her origami elephant.

Back with her familiar friend, the trusty sewing machine, Alex was mindlessly chain-piecing during quilting class. She had made it through the second-to-last step on her quilt blocks when she pondered the security footage Kane had shown her. She couldn't come up with an answer to Arthur's strange behavior. The footage matched up with Joey's account of the evening, but she couldn't help but wonder what else it revealed, what they hadn't shown her. In the security footage, Arthur had been behaving strangely about the ship throughout the night and early into the morning. *What was he doing?* Alex mindlessly puzzled over the bizarreness of it all.

This, much like Nona's mystery, was like no case she'd had before. As a criminal lawyer in NYC, she had seen just about everything, but the detective work had always been left to the police and often private investigators. This was all new to her. It seemed as though they should be similar jobs, but they were very different. Yes, she was familiar with asking the right questions, but as a defense attorney, her job was not collecting the evidence but throwing doubt on the evidence that was presented.

She had been assured that the ship's security personnel would be keeping an eye on Arthur's parents, so what was their connection? *Surely they didn't have anything to do with the death of their own son?*

Henrietta was heavy on her mind, too, both Henrietta, the grandmother's flower garden quilt, one of the ten quilts Nona had left behind as well as the person, presumably a human, named Henrietta, who they were soon to meet. Why had Nona felt the need to keep her secret from everyone on Spruce Street when Henrietta was so important to her that she'd made her one of her grandmother's flower garden quilts?

Alex had given out the named quilts to Nona's friends and family at the wake—her celebration of life, as she'd wanted it called. Alex had three mystery quilts left, each quilt containing two thousand or more small hexagons, all hand-stitched together and quilted completely by hand as well.

Alex was thinking about Nona and listening to the hum of machines and casual chatter in the room when Birdie's voice made her ears perk up. She recognized the woman's voice even before realizing she was in the room. Alex's ears perked up and she stopped sewing in time to hear Birdie telling Charlotte that they'd just got back from vacationing in Australia.

Wait! What is she doing in the quilting class today of all days? And why is she so calm while her son is . . . where? In the ice cream freezer? Alex heard Pete's voice in her head. *Surely, they have some sort of morgue on board the ship.*

12

ISLAND ARRIVAL

THE FOLLOWING MORNING, ALEX POURED HERSELF A GIANT glass of orange juice as the ship's captain announced their island arrival for the early afternoon over the loudspeakers.

Betty was her usual chipper self. "Are you excited to get off this ship? You look a little green this morning."

"Tell you the truth, Betty, I'm not really sure I want to get off this boat with . . . Arthur."

"We're not going to be with the body, Alex. We're going to meet Henrietta," Betty said with sass.

"It seems crude to have an autopsy done at a marine biology school, don't you think?" Alex asked without expecting an answer. "Although I am morbidly curious to find out if they really did put him in the freezer."

"Well, we will find out what this Henrietta quilt is all about," Betty said.

"Yes. There's that," Alex murmured and popped a few slices of bread into the toaster. As she sorted through the jellies, looking for the strawberry, she turned to Betty. "I really am sorry. I wasn't thinking about how you must feel. I know you have a stake in this, too, having been Nona's best friend."

"What do you think the keys go to?" Betty asked, ignoring Alex's statement.

"I can assume a door." Alex gave Betty a sly smile, though her attempt at humor flopped.

Alex spread the jam on her toast and sank her teeth into it while waiting for Betty to warm back up after Alex's failed joke.

"Could be a hidden treasure chest buried under the big red X! You know, with the tropical island and all," Betty mused and flashed Alex a goofy grin.

"Could be . . ." Alex said absently.

Betty put a slice of cranberry nut bread onto her plate. "I sure do miss my pies."

"Me too," Alex agreed and brought her toast and jam to a nearby table. She sat, motioning for Betty to join her.

"I haven't baked in days." Betty stared longingly at the small slice of breakfast bread.

Alex felt for her. She imagined going a week without baking for Betty was probably exactly how Alex felt about going without quilting for any length of time. Here Alex was being nourished, finally getting to quilt, while Betty was missing the activity that fed *her* soul.

"You know, Betty, I wanted to ask you last night if you could employ your *special people skills* to help us."

At that, Betty's eyes widened, her back straightened, and her face lit up with a magnificent grin. "I'll get Paul to help me," she said.

"Paul? From quilting class? Is that *who* you have been up to?"

Betty made the gesture of zipping her lips then said, "I don't kiss and tell."

Alex shook her head, trying to dispel that unwanted image.

Alex didn't hear anything else after that. She wanted to know more about the grimy old keys, their destination, and the three quilts Nona had left behind for unknown recipients, including Henrietta. She could assume that even if she didn't find all the answers on this trip, the other two quilts would likely take her on similar future adventures, though that didn't make her any less curious or impatient.

"Who . . ." Betty's mouth was moving, but Alex wasn't paying attention. "Alex? Are you listening?" Betty's voice finally snapped her from her reverie.

"Sorry, Betty, yes." She had unconsciously eaten both slices of toast, and Betty had apparently eaten her cake and already cleaned up.

"Who do you think Henrietta is?" Betty asked.

"I don't have the slightest idea." Alex shrugged. "You knew Nona better than I did. She was like a grandmother to me, and we had a friendship, but she didn't really share personal stuff with me over the years."

It saddened Alex every time she thought of how little she really had known about Nona. But as much as that pained her, she was still grateful Nona had raised her through her teenage years and into adulthood. Though impatient, she was grateful for this cruise and for the opportunity to find out who the quilts belonged to.

They cleared their plates and placed everything in the proper trays and trash bins before heading back to their rooms to get ready to disembark.

After breakfast, Alex readied herself for the crescendo of excitement this afternoon. With the trip to the island, she was sure she was finally going to solve the mystery of who Henrietta was. If nothing else made any sense yet, at least this part of the mystery would be solved.

Just after noon, she met up with Charlotte, Betty, and Celia at the elevator, which took them to deck 3. At the end of the corridor, there was an open section where you could get on and off the ship to participate in watersports and the like. Alex found it strange that none of those activities were offered. At least, she hadn't seen a mention of them in any of the reading materials. *Maybe watersports are for smaller ships like yachts rather than larger cruise ships.*

Celia squeezed Alex's arm as they stepped onto the tender, the small excursion boat that would take them to the island. "You ready?"

Alex leaned into Celia's squeeze. "Yes, I am, but I am still worried about Joey. I hate having to leave him behind," Alex replied.

"It's been an exhausting few months for all of us," Celia said. "You working on the case against Nona's murderer, you and me planning this trip, and Betty keeping the gossip mill running through it all."

Charlotte said, "I hope we are in for a *nice* surprise."

Nona had gone through all the trouble to book this cruise, get them to the school, buy the island . . . Alex could only speculate that this was it, the moment of truth. Alex had the quilt, Henrietta, inside a quilted bag that Betty had insisted she use.

She'd brought the keys and had the bag in her left hand, and she felt in the pocket of her shorts for the keys with her right hand. *Still there.* Alex naturally assumed they had something to do with the school or the island in some way, and she was anxious to find out what.

"I didn't get a chance to talk to you during quilting, Alex," Charlotte said.

The three younger women made their way to their seats. They sat down next to Betty, who waited expectantly for them to join her.

"What was up with Jane not showing up?" Charlotte asked.

"I don't know. I was in a zone. Honestly, I hadn't even realized she wasn't there. It is not like we really need her at this point."

"Did you see the addition to her wardrobe?" Betty asked. "The scarf around her neck, I mean. I wonder what she is hiding."

Alex and Charlotte exchanged a *Betty* look.

As the boat began to take off, Betty leaned closer and whispered, "They loaded the body before we got on so we wouldn't be disturbed by it."

Arthur's parents weren't in earshot, but Alex didn't want to risk them overhearing Betty and getting upset. "Shh, Betty. Please."

Betty scoffed audibly.

Alex peered at the unhappy couple, who sat a foot apart from one another on the same bench. They might as well have been strangers on a train for the way they ignored each other. The only thing they had in common was the look of contempt on their faces. Alex didn't like the uncomfortable feeling that arose at the sight. This was, after all, supposed to be a fun trip. *It isn't as though they planned this ill fate for their only son.*

The whole thing seemed straight out of a television drama show. It was obvious to her that Birdie and Ernesto should be allowed to go with the body to the lab, though the excursion originally had been intended for the Spruce Street group only.

But Alex couldn't reconcile the way the two parents were handling themselves, cold and unfeeling. Of all the cases she'd dealt with in her ten-year legal career, murder was the hardest on her since she came from a small town with very little crime, cocooned in the safety of their close-knit neighborhood on Spruce Street. The sins of the city always caused her to reflect on the human condition.

As they got closer to land, Madras Island, another tender, slightly bigger than the one they were on currently, passed by with the marine biology students heading for the cruise ship. The whole affair reminded Alex of one of those time-share deals where they give you a great deal and then try to sell you something. Only in this case, according to Celia, the cruise line was providing a discount to passengers who supported the marine biology school.

It took no more than ten minutes to get to the island, and the women hung back while staff shuttled Arthur off to an awaiting gurney at the dock, with his parents following somberly behind. The procession went left, toward an unpaved street, and Jane stood off to the right.

Alex, Celia, Charlotte, and Betty stepped off the ship. This wasn't like the dock where they'd set sail. It was no more than a small fishing pier.

Alex eyed Jane's Windsom uniform. The two-piece dress suit was perfectly paired, but the scarf around her neck was out of place and had Alex on alert. The scarf reminded Alex of when she had arrived back on Spruce Street, and Nona had used a scarf to cover her hair because she'd believed she was allergic to grass pollen.

"We have plenty of water and snacks if you get thirsty or hungry," Jane assured the group and handed Alex a water bottle, which she accepted.

She casually inspected the bottle and cap before taking a drink of water. The sun warmed her skin, and she was immediately refreshed when she sipped the water.

"Right this way, ladies," Jane said as she ushered them down the beach.

Once Alex and her friends had rounded a grove of exotic trees, a stately two-story white stone house came into view.

"Here we are," Jane said as she pointed to the front door.

The four women looked at each other curiously.

"Henrietta is a house?" Betty asked.

"No, no. You can go inside. I was told Henrietta would be inside awaiting your arrival," Jane said curtly.

Celia and Charlotte both looked to Alex to make the first move, but Betty was already walking toward the door. Luckily, she had sense enough to knock, which gave the other three time to catch up.

Celia and Charlotte held back a step, and Alex edged in front of Betty as the door opened.

13

HENRIETTA

"Good afternoon, ladies. I am Henrietta, and you must be Alex," said the tall woman, who looked to be in her mid-seventies.

She reached a long thin hand in Alex's direction. Alex gently shook it and was immediately warmed by the smell of cooking that wafted through the doorway. Her mouth watered, and before she had a chance to respond, Betty shot out her hand.

"Hi, I'm Betty, Nona's best friend."

"Welcome," Henrietta said awkwardly, shaking Betty's hand around Alex. "Come in. It is hot out there. I have the fans on, in here."

She motioned for the women to come inside. The Scooby Gang behind Alex pushed her through the front door, nearly knocking her off-balance. Alex reached out to the doorjamb to steady herself as they went past her, making her the last one through the door.

The interior of the house was like nothing Alex had seen in real life, only in the movies. The temperature was surprisingly chill. The curtains billowed as the overhead fan went round and round, circulating the cooler air with five symmetrical bronze blades that looked like giant leaves carved from stained wood. She was grateful for the cooler air.

The women stood in the foyer of the large home, gawking as they looked around. Alex could not help herself. Her eyes were wide. The carvings and woodwork that framed the area were mesmerizing and unexpected. Ahead of them to the left was an enormous hall tree to hang coats and umbrellas, with a long pew to sit and remove shoes and such. Just past those, a narrow straight staircase had been similarly treated with the wooden art. The entrance to the steps was surrounded by a round wooden arch that visually framed the stairs and the landing above like a picture frame, with a gorgeous crystal chandelier hanging in the center. To the right was a sitting room. Hand-crafted spindles fanned across the top of the over-sized opening, creating an archway of dark honey-colored woodwork.

Henrietta motioned for them to sit on a single oversized couch, several comfortable yet stylish chairs, and a giant ottoman. They all took a seat, with Alex sitting nearest to Henrietta.

"The captain told me you would be visiting today. This is such a treat for me. I generally don't get a lot of visitors. It's usually just me and Jinxy here." Henrietta lowered her hand to pick up the shiny black ball of fur. The cat purred obligingly as Henrietta gently scratched its head and smoothed its silky fur. Contented, the cat curled into a ball and went to sleep.

"You must be Charlotte?" Henrietta asked, looking directly at Charlotte. "You look just like Nona when she was younger."

Charlotte nodded, and her cheeks flushed. A tear formed at the corner of her eye.

"And Betty, Nona has told me so much about you. I hope you don't mind, but she passed along your recipe for stone fruit pie. I am sure mine isn't nearly as delectable as yours, but I do enjoy it on occasion!"

Betty sat silent for a minute, which was funny for Alex to see, and she couldn't help but grin. Tight-lipped, Betty replied with a simple, "Thank you."

Alex could see frustration in Betty's face. She wasn't sure if it was jealousy of Nona's relationship with this woman or a bit of anger that Nona had shared one of Betty's famous pie recipes.

"And, Celia, we have you to thank for arranging this trip! Blessings to you, my dear."

"You are most welcome, Henrietta. I apologize if we are all a little lost for words," Celia responded.

"Nonsense. No apologies necessary. I realize Nona's method of getting you here was a bit unconventional," Henrietta said and flicked her hand.

The small cat napping on her lap stirred. Henrietta immediately began scratching the feline's head. It rewarded her with a purr and went back to sleep.

"How rude of me. Would you all like some lemonade? Freshly squeezed. I made a fresh pitcher this morning. Nona shared Pam's recipe. You all like it nice and tart, from what I am told. There are sugar cubes here, though, if you need them."

Henrietta stood and set the little furball down on the couch next to Alex. Alex couldn't help but stroke the cat's glossy fur. It was deliciously soft and cuddly, a stark contrast to the mangy mutt, Kibbles, Alex had waiting on her to get home. She still had mixed feelings about the dog, though she had to admit she enjoyed her new sparky companion, even if she needed frequent grooming. It turned out that Kibbles was a female under all that gnarly fur, something Alex hadn't known until she had acquired the small pooch.

Alex was deep in thought when the other women

murmured affirmative responses to the offer of lemonade. Henrietta went through a swinging door behind her. She moved so fast Alex didn't even have a chance to offer a hand.

Celia leaned in to whisper, "What a sweet lady." Alex nodded, and Celia continued, "But I feel like we have so many more questions than we had a few minutes ago."

Alex chuckled nervously. *Yes, like what in the world? Are we in an episode of The Twilight Zone?*

"She seems to know all about us, and we know nothing of her," Charlotte whispered loud enough for the others to hear, but not so loud their hostess would overhear her from the other room.

She isn't wrong.

Henrietta came back in with a huge pitcher of lemonade.

"Can I help you with that?" Alex stood and asked this time.

"Yes, be a dear and grab the tray with the glasses and napkins. It's just through the door, on the counter."

Alex walked through the swinging door into a galley-style kitchen furnished with floor-to-ceiling cabinets painted white. A long braided rug covered the floor. The window at the far wall looked out on the beach, and she could see no end to the calm blue ocean beyond it. She picked up the tray from the counter and brought it out to the sitting area, as requested.

"Here, set that just here," Henrietta said, patting the ottoman. "We'll have some refreshing lemonade, and I'm sure you have a lot of questions for me. This must be most unusual for all of you."

Alex watched, mesmerized, as Henrietta poured lemonade into little tumblers and handed them out to the Spruce Street gang. Geesh, she really needed to stop referring to them as a gang.

"I am so sorry to hear about Nona's passing," Henrietta said regretfully. "She and I had become the best of friends over the years."

Years? Alex blinked, and Betty straightened in her seat.

Alex spoke up. "I am sorry that we didn't know about you to get in touch with you when she passed."

"Nonsense. How could we?" Betty asked coldly from Alex's right.

Alex could see what was going on here with Betty. She was indeed jealous.

"We knew nothing about you," Charlotte said, "until Alex found the quilt with your name on it then the letters Nona left us . . . and this mysterious . . . cruise." She choked out the last word.

Celia reached over to comfort Charlotte, pulled a handkerchief from her pocket, and handed it to her.

"Now, dear. Don't be sad. Nona loved you so. She was so proud of you." Henrietta turned to a side table to her right. "She sent me pictures regularly." She held up a picture of Charlotte and Nona at Charlotte's high school graduation.

"But how come she didn't tell us about you?" Charlotte moaned and sobbed.

"I am your grandaunt," Henrietta said. "Nona knew nothing about me for many years. She was married to my brother, you see, your grandfather." Henrietta produced a picture of what appeared to be Henrietta herself and her own brother, Charlotte's grandfather. Providing the women with a rare glimpse at Jack's dad, whom none of them had ever seen. She continued as they passed the picture between them. "That's me and my brother there, and this one is their wedding photo." She handed Charlotte another never-before-seen picture. "It was such a whirlwind romance. Our family knew little about Nona, and then when my brother died in the war . . ." Henrietta sighed and stared off into an old memory. "Things weren't like they are today. Back then, I mean."

"So this was your island before Nona bought it?" Celia asked

"Oh, heavens, no, dear. I came here after my husband passed away, just a few years ago. Nona thought I needed a job, something to do to keep me busy."

"That's just like Nona," Alex commented, remembering Nona's exact same words to Alex.

You need to work, Alex. Even though you are wealthy now and don't have to work, you must anyway. You will need something to work at every day.

"So, even though it was crazy for a seventy-year-old lady to move halfway across the world, I did because Nona asked me to," Henrietta said, chuckling and looking very amused and a bit proud of herself. "I came to look after the island and the kids, the students. They are like my grandchildren now. There's a full complement of staff here, of course. I am just the island granny, as they like to call me."

Well, that answers a few questions and makes room for a few more. Alex's heart was already warming to this sweet lady, but why had Nona kept her a secret from Charlotte and Jack? Surely they would have wanted to know about her sooner. Alex looked at Charlotte, and given the look on her face, Alex was right on that account.

Celia nudged Alex, disturbing her thoughts, and eyed the bag. Alex still had Henrietta, the quilt, in the quilted bag at her side.

"Henrietta, I believe this quilt is for you," Alex said as she pulled out the folded grandmother's flower garden quilt. "Nona left a few quilts. We don't yet know who the others belong to, but this one has your name on it."

Alex wrapped her arms around the teal quilt and squeezed

it to her chest before standing up. She stepped out from between the sofa and the ottoman to unfold it. Alex held it open for Henrietta to get a good look at it.

Betty begrudgingly stood to help Alex. She took one corner of the quilt to help hold it up. The lap-size quilt was hand-pieced from thousands of small hexagons in a myriad of teals, rich caramels and browns. Alex stared at the quilt. Nona had taken the colors of the ocean, these cruises, and this island and portrayed the color palette but with the traditional quilt blocks. It was overwhelming at that moment.

"My, my, I did not know she was working on one of these for me." Henrietta pulled a hankie from the pocket of the waist-apron that she wore over her cotton dress. She blotted her tears as she stood to admire the quilt.

"She made ten of them," Alex said. "One for each of her family members."

Alex took the corner from Betty and folded the quilt in half. She folded it until it was back to a size manageable to fit on a lap and handed it to Henrietta. Alex took her seat and saw that Celia was crying now, also. Alex leaned into Celia's side and stayed close to her friend, leaning on her for support and comfort.

They all sobbed and wiped their eyes and blew their now runny noses, all except for Betty, who remained stoic, if no longer appearing angry or jealous.

Remembering the keys in her pocket, Alex pulled them out. "Henrietta, I also have these keys that Nona left with the cruise tickets. Do you know anything about the keys or what they unlock?"

"I don't know about the skeleton key, but maybe you should try the other key on the door to Nona's room."

"Nona had a room here?" Alex looked around.

"Yes, of course. She stayed several times. We have a key to

the room also. We do still need to go in and freshen it up, dust and such. Here." She pulled a pile of keys out of the other pocket of her apron. Henrietta quickly found the key she was looking for and reached out for the key Alex had in her hand. As she held the keys up side by side, she said, "Look, yes, they match. Come with me. I will take you up to her room."

Henrietta glanced toward the stairs and stood up to lead Alex. Alex followed her hostess obligingly up to the second floor. The ornate wooden railing was smooth under her hand as she walked up the narrow steps. They reminded her of the back staircase at her own house at number 1 on Spruce Street. The top landing gave way to multiple rooms, two to each side and a bathroom in front of them. All of the doors were open, save for one, and there was furniture in them.

"Who else lives here?" she asked.

Henrietta smiled. "Just me, dear. Occasionally, a couple of students will stay here when there is an overflow at the school. Nona kept her room locked. She could be a very private person when she wanted to be."

"You're not kidding, Henrietta."

"Silly me. Of course you know this, seeing as she kept all this a secret." Henrietta pointed to the one door that was closed. "Just there. Go ahead. I will leave you to it," she said as she left Alex holding the key in front of the locked door.

14

MORE LETTERS

ALEX LET HERSELF IN AND WAS HIT BY A WAVE OF STALE AIR
that smelled like lilacs. She was instantly transported back to
Spruce Street with the two lilac bushes flanking the house.
Looking around for the flowers Alex couldn't find where the
familiar scent was coming from.

She stepped inside the room and closed the door behind
her. A picture of her and Nona at her graduation was on the top
of an antique oak dresser. She instinctively opened the top
drawer. Inside, she found the source of the lilac aroma in a small
satchel of dried flowers. Alex fumbled around in what could be
called a treasure drawer, finding a seashell, some sea glass, old
photos, a small pouch of toiletries, and some stationary. She
lifted the stationary, which had a large "N" in the upper right
corner. Under the papers lay some manila envelopes. Alex
removed the envelopes from the drawer. One had her own name
on it, and one read, "Do not open." Underneath that was a
journal.

She stepped back, set the "do not open" envelope on the
bed, and slid her finger through the seal on the envelope with
her name on it. Inside were some documents and a single piece

of parchment paper. Alex rubbed her finger over the hand-written letter. Nona's classic cursive was unmistakable. Alex had spent a lot of time reading and rereading Nona's previous letters that led her on this adventure.

Alex sat down on the four-poster bed and patted the quilt covering it. It wasn't a grandmother's flower garden quilt. It was a storm at sea quilt. Alex laughed as she realized why they were making a storm at sea quilt onboard the ship, but Alex had never seen Nona make any other quilt than the grandmother's flower garden quilts.

Alex,

> *If you are reading this, I was right to get my affairs in order.*

> *Surprise! Welcome to your island. Island number 19, to be exact. Fitting, don't you think? Henrietta and I came up with the name Madras. It means tightly woven cotton cloth. Also fitting. Keep the name, either way, or name it what you like.*

> *You're probably thinking I've gone off the deep end . . . again . . . but I assure you I haven't.*

> *My late husband, Jack's father, was a student of marine biology in his time before the war. Over the years, I have kept up with and supported various such programs around the world. When I found out that the students of Marine Biology Island 19 (MBI19 as the students like to call it) were struggling, I just had to help. At first, I sent monthly contributions. As an extreme effort to save the program, they decided to put this house up for auction, so naturally, it made sense for me to buy it, and I made them an offer they couldn't refuse.*

> *Several years ago, it became clear they needed a more permanent solution to their financial needs, so I bought the island. With your money. Thank you!*

> *In the last few years, Henrietta and I worked out a deal*

with the cruise ship to make an extra stop near the island. I'm sure the students are fleecing those rich passengers for everything they have as you read this.

Genius, isn't it! I hope this has been a grand adventure for our Spruce Street family.

Look after Joey as I have looked after you, although I'm sure he's already part of the family . . . Who knows? Maybe he will watch over number 1 when you visit the island in the future? Which I expect you to do.

Boy, I'd give anything to know how things worked out with Alastor. I bet he didn't come.

Anyway, Alex, my best girl, there's room on the island for you and Charlotte, Jack too, but since I used your money to buy the island, it is yours to do with as you see fit.

Maybe you'll marry that handsome investigator and retire here someday . . . Yes, I knew you had feelings for him. Don't try to deny it. The way you talked about him reminded me of your mother and how she talked about your father. Both good men.

There are documents and another envelope. It says Do not read, but you will know when it is the right time to open it. Henrietta knows everything about the island and will have any information you need when you're ready for it. I hope you will find comfort with her, since I am gone. She is a dear woman. I know you will love her as I did. She has become like a sister to me.

Look after my students, too, but most of all, enjoy this oasis. You deserve it!

~ Love, Nona

Alex clutched the letter to her heart and wept silently. She stood up to look for a tissue. The envelopes, forgotten in her lap, fell to the floor, along with the journal, which thudded on the wooden floorboards. Alex bent, retrieved the hardcover book, and smoothed the edges, feeling guilty that she had dropped it.

Standing in the middle of the sparsely furnished room, she remembered her friends downstairs awaiting her return. She gave the room one more once-over and slipped out, closing and locking the door behind her.

Betty's and Henrietta's voices rose up the stairs, louder than the others.

"Since I am the island granny, the students tell me everything about what's going on here on the island, and I heard the students will be doing a most unusual procedure today."

"I heard they were going to be doing an autopsy on the young man," Betty said. "Are they equipped for that? I mean, does marine biology really translate to humans?"

The room quieted as Alex turned the corner, holding the envelopes and journal.

Alex took her seat on the sofa. Two fresh boxes of tissues had appeared while she had been upstairs. Looking around, she spotted a few hexagon-themed quilted items she thought had been made by Nona. She reached for a doily made of hexagons on the side table next to the sofa.

"Did Nona make this?" Alex asked.

"Oh, yes, she was always making these little hexagons." Henrietta stroked the doily as well.

"She left another letter." Alex held up the envelopes.

Charlotte sat bolt upright. "Does it say why she didn't tell us about Henrietta?"

"No, unfortunately, it answers only a few questions and leaves me with more." Alex reached over Celia and handed the letter she had read upstairs to Charlotte.

The room was silent as Charlotte read the letter. Moments

later, when she had finished reading, she sat still and quiet before asking, "Can you tell us more, Henrietta?"

Charlotte stood and handed the letter to Betty.

While Betty read, Henrietta explained, "She wanted to, but you know how she was. Stubborn and private." Henrietta crossed herself and whispered a prayer. "It was hard for her to talk about personal things. It was a sad time in her life. She had lost her husband to the war. My brother, he was the love of her life. Even so many years later . . . Well, I am a little younger, so I wasn't privy to all that went on, but from what I understand, when she showed up pregnant, my parents didn't handle it well. They had lost their only son, you know. You would think they would want to hold on to their grandson, but they just didn't want to have anything to do with her or the baby. It didn't make sense to me, but as I said, I was just a young girl at the time.

"Eventually, when I was old enough, I started searching for her, and as you can imagine, she was still holding the grudge against our family all those years later. She didn't warm up to me at first, but I kept trying. Over the years, we started to become friendly, meeting up occasionally between assignments, and then finally we became more. Sisters."

All the women reached for tissues.

Henrietta looked at Charlotte. "She missed your grandfather so much. It wasn't until she met Liam that her heart began to heal." She held her hand over her own heart. "We started doing all of this good work for the students, the island, and so much more. I am sure you will learn in time."

"But how could she have orchestrated all of this?" Charlotte asked. "She could not have known she was . . ." Charlotte couldn't finish the words.

Alex understood what she was asking. She had asked herself the same question a dozen times.

"No, I think her plans began years ago. I believe all of this

—" She held her hands up, holding the reality of their current situation metaphorically in her hands. "She was putting her life and priorities in order. She had realized she had lost so much time already, and her life was finite." Henrietta dabbed her handkerchief at the corner of her eye and then continued. "Sure, on the surface, she had an exciting life, some of which she shared with me, and of course she loved all of you fiercely, but she never found her true love again. Until she met Liam." Henrietta pointed to the diary in Alex's hands. "I'm sure you will find many answers there . . . And many new questions as well. She was truly an extraordinary woman. I can only imagine the life that my brother would have had with her."

At that thought, Henrietta finally broke and let her tears come. Alex leaned toward Henrietta's chair, put her hand gently over Henrietta's, and was rewarded when she returned the squeeze and held on to Alex's hand.

After they *all* had a good cry, Alex asked, "Do you know more about Liam? Nona left a quilt for him, one of the mysteries yet to be solved when we get back to Spruce Street."

"I'm confident you will find those answers in the journal. I have not read it, of course. I do not know what it says, but I find it hard to believe she would not have written about him." Henrietta stood up and straightened herself and her apron. "I think Alex and I should head over to the lab and meet the staff and maybe check on the status of things. It is nearly time to head back to the ship," she said, looking at a dainty metal watch on her wrist. "We'll drop you ladies off at the dock to wait. I am sure they will have some more refreshments for you."

In the school building, Henrietta showed Alex to the wing that housed the lab and offices. There, they found Mimi.

"Alex, this is Mimi. She is the lab manager. Mimi, this is Alex, Nona's, ah, granddaughter? I am sorry, dear. Is that right?"

"Granddaughter is fine," Alex assured them and reached out her hand to shake Mimi's. "It's nice to meet you, Mimi."

"You as well, Alex," Mimi said cautiously while Alex looked around.

"Mimi, it looks like you're studying botany here, not marine biology."

"I dabble. This is just my office. I will take you to the lab. The students are working on their findings now. We released the young man's body back to his parents."

"Do you know if he died from the slip and fall?" Alex asked but quickly realized Mimi had no obligation to share those details with her.

"Technically, yes, he did die from hitting his head on the deck. Well, the deck chair, to be exact."

Henrietta interrupted and backed up a step. "Well, I am going to leave you two to your work. It was so very nice to finally meet you in person, Alex."

Alex stepped forward to meet her, and Henrietta leaned in and gave Alex a good squeeze. She was surprisingly strong.

"Call me when you get back or if you have any more questions. Mimi will give you all the contact information." Henrietta smiled and then grimaced. "I can make other arrangements if you decide you want to live here."

"That is not necessary, Henrietta. It is your home. We can talk more about it when I get back to Spruce Street."

"Thank you, dear."

"It would be great for you to come to Salem and stay with us and meet Jack."

"Yes, I would like that very much. It is too bad he didn't come on the cruise. Give him my best, will you?"

"I will, Henrietta, and thank you again for your hospitality. We will be in touch real soon."

After Henrietta left, Alex turned back to Mimi, who had her face over a microscope.

She pulled out a glass slide and said, "Here, look. We found a white chalky substance. This is guano, otherwise known as poop."

"Yes, I know what guano is." Alex smiled. "But what was bat poop doing on a cruise ship?" She wrinkled her brow in confusion.

"No, that is a common misconception. Most people think it only applies to bats, but guano refers to seabird excrement as well."

"Okay, that makes much more sense. We did find an enormous pile of it on the deck." Alex widened her eyes to portray the enormity of the pile. "Joey and I almost slipped on it ourselves."

"It is a bit strange that there was such a big, er, fresh . . . pile." Mimi giggled, showing her young age. She had to be at least ten to fifteen years younger than Alex was. "I think the mystery that needs to be solved is what led up to his death? Sure, he could have slipped on poop, fallen, and hit his head, and we could wrap that up in a bow and be done with it," Mimi said, her eyes bright with curiosity.

Alex cocked her head at the strange little woman. It was an odd thing to say, but Alex couldn't help but like her quirkiness and charm.

"Sorry. I don't get out of the lab much, and I love a good mystery!"

Mimi glanced toward the desk. Alex's eyes followed and narrowed in on a book. It was a cozy mystery from the same author she was reading.

"What I mean is what about all of the other details that lead up to the death?" Mimi asked.

Alex looked back to Mimi and she motioned for Alex to follow her to the actual lab, through a door at the back of Mimi's office. Alex had to duck under a hanging plant near the door.

Mimi stopped at the first worktable. "We found these scratches all over his legs and found some fibers and hairs . . ." She handed Alex a small stack of photographs showing the evidence she was referring to.

"Should you be showing this to me?" Alex asked.

"Well . . ." Mimi said in a singsongy voice. "Technically? You own this lab." She smiled a rueful smile at Alex.

First the house, then the island, and now she owned the lab too.

"We can get to that bit later," Alex replied.

Mimi nodded. "It appears that anaphylactic shock caused the disorientation."

"*Again?*" Alex interrupted.

Mimi gave her a questioning look.

Alex waved her hand and said, "Never mind."

Mimi continued looking at Alex expectantly.

"Sorry, it is just that Nona essentially died of that, too, but that person is in jail."

Curiosity satisfied for the moment, Mimi said, "However . . ."

"There's more?"

"Well, you know he hit his head, but I don't have the resources to determine if that was the actual cause of death." Mimi picked up another picture and showed Alex. "There was a scraping puncture wound on his foot, which had nothing to do with his death but is more of an oddity."

Alex reluctantly looked at the photo. *Oh, that is an awfully small puncture wound. What could Arthur have stepped on that—*

Alex winced as she remembered her seam ripper, covered in blood on the floor of the cabin. *Arthur must have stepped on it. Should I tell Mimi?*

Misunderstanding Alex's hesitation, Mimi explained further, "It was metal and sharp, whatever it was. Maybe you can look for clues near the scene or around his last known whereabouts?"

"I'm pretty sure I know exactly what it is, Mimi. I am just not sure what it all means yet. The cut on his foot, do you think it could have been from a seam ripper? Do you know what that is?"

"Ha, of course I know what a seam ripper is, Alex. You don't think every student here has not been taught to quilt?" She giggled. She really was cute, and thinking that made Alex immediately feel old. "I wouldn't have guessed it, but now that you mention it, that is exactly what it could be from.

"Then, there is the rash. I'm no human rash expert, but this will most likely be classified as a severe allergic reaction, though I suspect it doesn't have anything to do with food. See here, on his forearm? We took bloodwork and skin samples. We also pulled some microscopic hairs from the area, but it is going to take a few hours for us to figure out what it is and what it all means," Mimi finished and snapped off her latex gloves.

"So, do you think it was intentional or an accident?"

Before Mimi could answer Alex's question, a group of students filed in through a door at the opposite side of the lab. They chatted happily, with their bags, posters, and props in tow. They couldn't have been much younger than Mimi herself, save for one man at the back of the pack who looked to be in his fifties.

"Here's the team, now. Let's see how they did aboard the ship."

"Mimi, they wanted us to tell our guests 'all aboard.'"

"That was fun," someone said excitedly from the back of the pack.

"How did you do?" Mimi asked.

"Oh, this ship was a winner! Not only did we get next year's scholarships secured, but I think we also got enough to get the submarine running again!"

"Eeeee," another one shrieked. "So exciting!"

"Well done!" Mimi congratulated the ponytail-bobbing young lady.

"He was so dreamy," a dark-haired girl in the back cooed.

"Wow. A submarine?" Alex asked.

"Not like ones you see on television. It's much smaller than that," Mimi replied.

Alex nodded. "May I use the ladies' room, Mimi?"

"Sure, Alex. Just turn to the right, and it is at the end of the hallway."

"Thank you. I will leave you to celebrate. I'll be right back."

"Light switch is on the left as you go through the door," Mimi called out as Alex walked away.

Alex traveled the long, dimly lit corridor. The walls were ocean blue and beautifully painted with vignettes of tropical island beach themes with a plethora of sea life playing in the water. The end of the hall was a "T," with the bathroom door straight ahead as Mimi had said. To the left, an emergency exit sign hung overhead, about a hundred feet away, and to the right was pitch blackness.

The ladies' room was sparse and rundown. She would have expected this in an old gym locker room at an abandoned school. Looking at the frame painted on the wall where a mirror would normally be, she turned on the cold tap. Her skin was tacky with sweat. She could at least wash off her hands and lower arms. The frigid water was soothing.

Alex looked up at a faint knocking. The fan overhead was off-kilter as it rambled around and around slowly. The cool air circling down raised gooseflesh on her skin. She shivered and then ran the cold water over her hot skin with her hands, causing a fresh eruption. Alex wondered for a moment where the terms *gooseflesh* or *goose bumps* came from. She would have to get these kids a proper cooling system to keep the air at a steady temperature, possibly the wall-mounted type but more likely a complete system.

Alex bent her head and splashed her face with the soothing, crisp tap water. As she raised her head, she sniffed, smelling something spicy in the air. Before she had time to react, someone grabbed her shoulder. She struggled and then something covered her mouth. A searing pain shot through her temple, and a moan escaped her before she slipped into darkness.

Alex opened her eyes to find Celia, Mimi, and a peculiar mop of something blue staring down at her.

"What...what happened?" Alex struggled with the formation of her own questions "How?" She looked around wildly. "How long?"

"Easy, now," Celia said as Alex tried to get up off the floor.

"Are you okay?" Mimi asked. "What happened here? We came to check on you and found you lying here out cold."

"Are you all right, lady?" came from above her.

Mimi shushed the girl with the huge head of blue hair.

Ignoring the questions, Alex rubbed the side of her head, still dazed.

"Here, let us help you up," Celia said. She and Mimi both pulled Alex up to her feet, one on each of Alex's arms.

"Whoa," Mimi said as Alex wobbled, gaining her footing. "Steady, girl."

"What is that smell? Gross!" another student said upon entering and popped her head over the women.

"I don't know," Alex said groggily. "Someone grabbed me on the shoulder and covered my mouth with a rag or something. I think I hit my head. I . . . It happened so fast." She absently put her hand on her own shoulder.

"You felt someone grab you? Did you see or hear anything?" Celia asked.

"It smelled sweet," she said, putting a hand over her mouth.

"Chloroform?" the head of blue asked. "Was someone trying to abduct or kill you? I have only seen that in the movies."

"Maybe. I don't know? I don't think chloroform works like they portray it in the movies. Who else is here?" Alex asked.

"No one. It's just us," Mimi said quietly.

"I felt a hand on my shoulder. No..." Alex shook her head and yelped. She raised her hand to the searing pain. Her hair was wet. Blood. When she pulled her hand away, she stared at the wet red stain on her fingertips. "Well, it was a hand, but it felt padded . . ."

"Like a glove," Celia finished Alex's sentence.

They looked each other in the eyes. They both knew a glove could only mean one thing.

"Arthur's parents," Alex murmured.

15

A PAIN IN MY HEAD

"But Birdie and Ernesto went back to the ship with the body," Mimi said, looking at her watch. "Over a half an hour ago now . . . I watched them leave with one of the ship's security officers."

"Where *is* that darn security team when we need them?" Celia said. "We should have brought Officer Mark."

Alex frowned and winced again. She was leaning against the wall and used it for leverage to push herself straight and take a step forward.

"Let's get you back to the ship. The doctor can have a look at your head. Can you walk?" Celia asked, taking Alex's arm on her own.

"Yes, I am fine," Alex said, but her vision blurred slightly, and she grabbed a hold of a nearby chair to steady herself.

"Whoa," Mimi said. "Easy, girl."

Alex imagined Mimi must talk to the marine life exactly like this, and she chuckled.

"What could be funny?" Celia said.

"Never mind. Let's get onto that boat."

"Celia wrote down your numbers for me, and I will call you

once I know anything," Mimi said. "I mean I'll call the captain with a full report," she added with a coy smile and an exaggerated wink.

"You had better text us. I don't think we're able to get phone calls," Celia called back as she and Alex headed down the beach to the ramshackle dock where the small ship awaited them, along with Betty and Charlotte.

"What happened, ma'am?" the bulky security officer asked.

"She was attacked," Celia replied. "Where were you? You had better keep everyone away from us until we figure out who attacked her."

"I-I..." he stammered and lowered his head. Looking back up at her with renewed confidence, he said, "Yes, ma'am, I will." He turned and hurried onto the boat.

"Jeesh, where's he going now? He could have at least helped us onboard," Betty said.

Charlotte helped Betty onto the tender.

Celia tried to get Alex situated.

"Stop fussing over me," Alex said.

With a shaky laugh, Betty said, "You sound like Nona." She collapsed on the bench beside Alex. "Are you sure you are okay? The ship's personnel are useless."

"They definitely are not very helpful, Betty. I'm going to need some aspirin."

As the boat took off, Celia handed Alex some aspirin that she'd fished out of the emergency kit overhead. She sat next to Alex and went over the conversation she'd had with Mimi before they had found Alex in the bathroom. "Mimi said she thought the small fibers were hairs."

"Like human hair?" Alex grimaced at the thought while fiddling with an invisible thread on her skirt.

"No, plant, actually," Celia replied, "a rare and potentially deadly plant, though Mimi said she has never actually seen one in person. She gave me a list of a few of the possible botanical suspects." Celia chuckled. "Deadly nightshade, Sally."

Alex guffawed at Celia's reference to the popular 90s animated film. "Funny. Could it be?"

"Not likely to be nightshade, at least according to Mimi."

The ship was going at a good clip now.

"Oh, no. My bag." Alex reached out toward the island shrinking in the distance.

"I have it here. Don't worry. You left it in Mimi's office," Celia said, removing it from over her shoulder and handing it back to Alex.

"I nearly forgot about it. The letters and the journal are in there."

"Not to worry. It's safe."

Alex clutched the bag to her chest and stared out onto the water. She replayed the day's events in her mind. "It seemed like Mimi had a pretty extensive botany collection in her office," she said absentmindedly.

"Side project." Celia raised her voice over the wind. "You should think about helping her expand the school to include botany."

"Already making a mental list," Alex whispered, forced a smile, and then closed her eyes.

After the island excursion, she had some answers but mostly more questions, the biggest being was there something nefarious about Arthur's death? And now, who was responsible for hitting her over the head? And why?

Her backside vibrated, and she jumped in her seat then groaned from the headache pounding at her temples. She pulled out her phone to read the text message.

Lex, you OK? Check in, please.

A perfectly timed text from Hawk, which immediately had an effect on her. Her heart rate slowed, and her face flushed.

Did he already know what had happened? *Impossible.* Alex slipped the phone back into her pocket. *Later.* As much as she wanted to talk to him, the increasing drumbeat in her head made it impossible to think coherently. She closed her eyes and prayed the headache, in combination with the choppy sea, wouldn't make her nauseous.

The phone vibrated in her pocket a second time, and she couldn't help herself. She pulled out the phone to check the text from Hawk, but this message was from an unknown number, not a regular phone number like the last one but a five-digit number.

Do not put yourself in harm's way

A mysterious text from an unknown number. How convenient.

She typed fast and hit send. *Who is this?*

She stared at the screen, willing it to respond with an answer.

Alex had finally given up on watching for a reply to the text when they arrived back at the *Tranquility*. Safely back on the ship, Alex stopped just outside the doors to the private lounge. She overheard Betty and Pete in their own speculative conversation, similar to the one Alex had been having with herself.

"My money is on the mother. What kind of mother just shows up to quilting class after her son dies on board a cruise ship?"

Thanks to Betty, it wasn't long before the whole Spruce Street family converged on Alex inside the lounge. *I don't know how she does it.*

Pete brought everyone up to speed on his conversation with Betty and his opinions of Birdie and Ernesto.

Lucy said, "Well, regardless of which one of them may have ulterior motives, I say we need to keep clear of both of them."

Ignoring Lucy's statement, Betty continued to speculate. "We don't know why Arthur was acting weird that night or why his parents would kill him."

"What about all of the things Arthur was saying?" Lucy asked. "I mean, what did folks hear him say when he was, ah, streaking across the ship?"

"'Help me,' something about a 'broom,' the word 'don't' and 'warn you,'" Alex replied to Lucy.

"I think he was trying to warn *you*, Alex."

Pete chimed in, "Broom has to be a mistake. Maybe he was saying 'room'?"

"I don't know. I can't think right now." Alex groaned. Then, she frowned. "Hey, why are you looking at *me* like that? I'm the one who got hit over the head a couple hours ago."

Acting like the cat that caught the canary, Betty mused, "It's probably an affair. I overheard them arguing in the corridor this morning."

"What did you hear?" Lucy handed Alex some ice rolled up in a linen napkin.

"'Why did you bring our son on this cruise. It is all your fault,'" Betty quoted.

"Who said that?" Celia asked, lowering her voice to a whisper.

"The wife said that to the husband," Betty said in a low voice also and leaned closer to the group.

"So, what does that mean?" Pete questioned and crossed his arms. "I don't see how that means an affair or tells us which one is the killer."

"I couldn't hear the whole conversation, but I heard her say 'Bimbo' too," Betty said, puffing her chest, proud as a peacock that *she* had solved the case. "That's why I know it was an affair."

"Not so fast, Betty." Alex put up a hand to Betty's meddling remarks. "That doesn't give us the motive of why. Why would either of them want to harm their son?"

"Oh, no!" Betty exclaimed. "You think someone was sleeping with the young man?" Her eyes went wide in horror, and then she covered her mouth with her hand.

"What?" the group asked collectively and stared at Betty.

Betty shrugged, recovering from her surprise. "What?"

"What about what was said led you to *that* conclusion?" Alex furrowed her brow.

"Well, the kid, I mean the young man, Arthur, was killed, and someone was having an affair. If it was the father having an affair, the mother wouldn't have killed the kid. If it was the mother having the affair, the father wouldn't have killed the kid, right?" Betty proclaimed.

Pete smirked. "Okay, she does have a vague point there, Alex."

"Unless it was the father having an affair and the son knew about it. The father would have killed Arthur to shut him up," Alex mused. "I can't even believe I am entertaining this wild theory. It is giving my headache a headache."

"Same goes for the mother?" Pete mumbled and shrugged one shoulder.

Lucy, the only voice of reason in this whole conversation, cleared her throat. "Was the autopsy performed? Did you find out anything while you were on the island?"

Celia and Alex explained what they had learned on the island from Mimi and her team.

"Someone needs to tell the captain there is a killer on the ship," Celia said.

"Okay, Captain Obvious," Betty said.

All eyes shot to Betty.

"Sorry. I got caught up in the moment. Sometimes, this seventy-five-year-old mouth has a mind of its own." Betty shrugged innocently and sat in a nearby chair.

Following Betty's lead, Alex sat across from her and said, "I would hope by now the captain has the smarts to know he has a serious problem, but I am not sure if he realizes there might be something more sinister going on."

Something was niggling at her subconscious. If only she could pull back the veil in her mind to see whatever it was that she already knew or was missing. *I'm certain I would easily remember if it weren't for this darn headache.*

"Wait. Are you sure they didn't say Bambino?" Pete let out a booming laugh right by her head.

Alex winced and sighed. "I will go speak to the captain. So much for resting . . . or quilting later. I'm going to check on Joey first, though." She stood up too quickly, and Celia instinctively reached out a hand to support her. Alex steadied herself, holding on to the table.

"Not with that theory?" Celia asked.

"No, I will think of something on the way over. I can always chat him up about Nona, get him talking. I assume there is a story to be told, now that we know Nona took this trip to the island multiple times, and then I'll see where the conversation goes from there."

"What are we going to do in the meantime?" Betty asked.

"We had better get dressed," Pete said.

"Be serious, Pete." Lucy swatted at her husband insincerely.

"I am, my love. We have the mingles gala tonight and are expected to be dressed in our finery in..." He looked down at his watch. "An hour."

"Ugh . . ." Alex groaned again. "Definitely not!"

"We have to go, Alex," Betty said.

"She's right, Alex," Pete agreed. "We—"

"We have to talk to all the other guests," Betty interrupted him. "At least, as many as we can. It will be our best opportunity to get the information we need to figure out who killed Arthur."

"And who is having the affair. I think we can assume it is one of the parents," Alex replied.

16

MINGLES SHMINGLES

Down the corridor, Alex stopped at Joey's cabin and gave a quick double tap on the door.

"Alex," Joey said as he opened the door to peek out. "Thank goodness it's you. I have been pacing the room for hours." His gaze met the floor, and he sagged against the wall and let out a huge breath. "I was about to start climbing the walls."

"We're back now. Come with me. I want to keep an eye on you." Alex urged him forward and out of the room. "I need to go talk to the captain. I'm still a little fuzzy, but it is only one flight up. We can take the stairs."

"Fuzzy? From what? What's happened, Alex?"

"Nothing for you to worry about. Someone hit me on the head while we were on the island. Knocked me out cold for a beat."

"Nothing to worry about? What do you mean, Alex? You are the only person here that I can trust," he said to her with pleading eyes.

Alex put a comforting hand on his arm. "It is going to be okay." Entering the stairwell, she said, "And you can trust our other Spruce Street friends too."

Coming out of the stairwell, Alex plowed into Kane.

"Whoa," he said, grabbing her by the arm. "Why in such a hurry, Miss Bailey?"

"My apologies," she said, composing herself. "We're headed to see the captain."

"You really shouldn't be meddling in the investigation," he said with a condescending glare.

"I am not meddling in anything," she replied in a firm tone to let him know she meant business. He didn't intimidate her at all. "I am a witness, *and* I was attacked today. I would say that puts me right in the thick of it."

"I saw you and your friend on the security footage. I don't know how you got into that room, but I'm telling you to steer clear from here on out." Kane said and abruptly walked away.

When they entered the bridge, Alex and Joey met Staff Captain Jim James.

"The cap is on his break," he told Alex casually.

Once Alex explained why she was looking for him, he confided that someone was watching Arthur's parents.

Since talking to the captain was a bust, Alex decided there wasn't much else to do but go back to their cabins and get ready for the mingles evening. Alex and Joey entered the stairwell to return to the lounge, Alex heard a thump, as if something heavy had hit the floor below them.

Alex put her finger to her mouth and held out her hand to stop Joey from going any farther. "Shh, did you hear that?" She pointed down. The stairwell led back to the lounge and the corridor where their cabins were. "Wait here. I'll check it out."

"I'm not letting you go by yourself, Alex. I'm definitely coming with you."

"Okay, but stay behind me and be quiet."

They tiptoed down a couple more stairs. Nothing at the first landing halfway down. They crept around the railing and down the last half flight of stairs, and Alex peeked through the door.

"Nothing there," she said, looking to the right.

The view to the left was a different story. Alex swung the door open and rushed down the hallway.

"What is it?" Joey asked, following on Alex's heels.

"It's Jane," Alex called out over her shoulder.

Jane sat on the floor with her head slumped forward.

Alex squatted next to her. "Jane, are you all right?" Alex gave her a shake on the shoulder, and adrenaline began to flood Alex's system when she didn't answer.

"Check for a pulse, Alex."

Alex was about to when Jane started to stir.

"Oh, good grief. She's alive." Joey leaned against the wall and breathed out a huge sigh. He ran his hand through his hair, causing it to stand up. "My heart is racing so fast. Geez, Alex, I don't think I could handle it if someone else died on this cruise."

"What . . . What happened?" Jane mumbled as she came to. "You!" She said and tried to get up.

Alex encouraged her to remain where she was, but Jane insisted on standing. Alex stood with her, holding on to Jane's elbow to provide support. Jane yanked her arm away from Alex. Unsteady on her feet, Jane began to teeter, and Joey grabbed her other arm to steady her.

"We found you here," Alex answered.

"What happened to you?" Joey asked.

Jane's scarf had loosened from her neck, revealing faint red marks on both sides of her neck.

What is going on here? Was she strangled?

"Jane, did someone try to hurt you?" Alex asked.

Jane rubbed the back of her head in confusion. She teetered again.

Alex said, "Let's go find a place to sit."

"No, I have to go. She tried to kill me!"

"Who?" Alex asked.

"Never mind. I'm fine. I have to go. Don't touch me. Leave me alone." Jane glared at Alex.

"I . . ." Alex was about to urge her to get some medical attention when Jane turned and walked away.

Alex and Joey stood watching her walk in the opposite direction. Jane shuffled her skirt and tucked in her blouse, wobbling slightly, bumping into the walls, and holding them to get herself steady.

"Don't follow me. I said leave me alone," Jane yelled back at them.

Alex turned to Joey and realized he was holding something. "What do you have there?"

He shrugged. "Must be what knocked her out."

"Who is trying to kill Jane? And why?" Alex whispered.

Joey opened his hand. "It's a woman."

Alex looked at Joey holding the quilting tool.

"If we didn't know it from this, she said 'She tried to kill me.'" Joey said and held it up.

Alex put out her hand to take the oblong wooden quilting tool. She inspected the piece of wood. "It's a clapper," she said to Joey. "Someone must have grabbed it from the quilting room. It is used to hold in heat and flatten out your seams while ironing."

Joey looked back at her with a blank stare.

"Never mind. Look. No blood." She held up the clapper. "That's a good sign. I'm sure Jane will be all right, whatever is going on with her."

Alex wasn't so sure, though, despite her words. *Has she been a victim twice now? Someone came back to do the job a second time? It might explain why she was nowhere to be found at the last quilt meeting. Hiding out, maybe? But from who and why?*

"Who's next, Alex?" Joey asked.

"I don't know. Come, we need to get dressed up." Alex motioned Joey to follow her. "And get to the bottom of all this!"

Less than a half hour later, Alex made her way to the yacht club. She had loosely braided her hair to one side to cover the knot she could feel on her head and changed into a simple off-white, knee-length sheath dress that she had purchased specifically for the trip. The black Tahitian pearl necklace was the perfect complement to the high neckline of the dress. Nona had given her the string of pearls for her graduation, and she wore them quite frequently. She didn't own very much jewelry—a few pieces that had been handed down over the generations that she never had the occasion to wear; a pair of diamond studs that an ex had given her, that she wore in her ears most days; and a pair of pearl earrings that she had bought herself to match the neck-lace. With the matching pearl ensemble, she was as glamorous as she was going to get on this cruise.

She took a deep breath and put on a smile as she walked into the lion's den. Everyone sparkled from head to toe: women with sequined evening gowns and baubles on their shoes, hands, necks, and in their hair and men with their shoes shined, ties tacked, and cufflinks flashing as they moved their arms in animated conversation.

As she stood and watched the passengers, she felt good and almost happy, at least better than she had felt since Arthur had died. Momentarily distracted she forgot that she was here to collect information and instead felt like she was here to relax and enjoy herself. Alex beamed when she saw Joey headed her way, in a white dress shirt and simple solid-black tie. She was glad he had traded his khaki cargo pants for gray slacks.

"You look nice, Alex," he said shyly.

"As do you," she said simply, trying not to embarrass him.

"Shall we?" He held out his arm for her like a proper gentleman.

She smiled. Though there was no familial relation, she felt motherly and was proud of him. Kind and handsome, Joey was going to make a good husband to a lovely girl someday.

"I think I need a drink first," she said.

"A little liquid courage?" he asked her jokingly, and just like that, the dynamic was of sister and little brother again.

Soon, Alex stood facing the bar and sipped her summer breeze cocktail while Joey went off to find the others.

Jon Draper walked up to the bar, standing close to her he faced the crowd. He extended his hand. "May I have a dance?"

She took his hand, not knowing what had come over her, and he whisked her onto the dance floor. They danced close enough for her to breathe in his earthy scent. He pulled her close, with one hand on the small of her back he held her other hand between them and close to his chest. It was a little more romantic than she had bargained for, but she found herself drawn to him and stared into his eyes. She found him genuinely interesting and very charismatic.

"You look gorgeous," he whispered.

"Thank you."

"Is everything all right, Alex?" he asked, moving slowly around the dance floor.

"Sorry. It has been a long day. I was attacked on the island," she said, and he pulled her in closer. At the worried look on his face, she said, "I'm fine. Just a bump on the head, thankfully."

"Do you know who it was?"

"Well, it could have been one of only a few people," she said, looking into his eyes as they swayed slowly to the rhythm of the music. She wasn't sure why she was telling him about the case and her suspicions, but she couldn't help herself. "I doubt it was Mimi, Henrietta, or anyone from Spruce Street," she said absently.

He gave her a puzzled look, and she briefly explained who Henrietta and Mimi were.

"So it must have been Jane, Ernesto, or Birdie," she said, following his lead on the dance floor.

"I thought Jane was the quilting liaison. Why would she try to hurt you?"

"I don't think it was her. I think someone has attacked her . . . at least once, if not twice."

A fierce, protective look shot across his eyes.

"I am okay. I can take care of myself, but we have to get to the bottom of this. With one *murder*," she said questioningly, "and at least two attacks, I'm not sure who is safe or who will be next."

"I think I have a piece to your puzzle," he said, holding her gaze. He stared so long she nearly forgot he was speaking. "I saw the mother, Birdie, having a fit. She was screaming and throwing things off her balcony into the ocean. I was surprised that she didn't get caught, but I chalked it up to bereavement or a marital spat over the loss of their son."

"What did she throw overboard?" Alex stopped moving.

"Just some of her husband's things . . . things from the room. I was on the deck above so I couldn't hear the argument, but I had a clear view."

Alex stood waiting for him to tell her more. He let go of the hand he had been holding, and with his other hand still on the small of her back, he urged her to an empty table nearby.

Once seated, she asked again, more impatiently this time, "What was she throwing overboard?"

"Some gloves, a bagged plant, some papers."

"How did you know it was a plant?" Alex asked.

"It came out of whatever it was wrapped in when she hurled it off the ship. I watched the plastic float on the wind for a while. She was gone by the time I looked back."

Alex knew instantly what it was. "Evidence," she said. "Birdie was destroying the evidence."

"How are those things evidence? Evidence of what?"

"The plant, the gloves . . ."

"I still don't understand," he said with a patient tone in his voice.

She explained the dangerous plant fibers that Mimi had found on Arthur's body. "I don't know exactly what it means yet, but I will figure it out."

"Well, that explains the gloves," he said matter-of-factly. "I was wondering why the guy was wearing gloves on a cruise to a tropical island."

Betty abruptly sat beside Alex. "Hi. Alex, I need to talk to you."

"Whatever it is, Betty, you can say it in front of Jon."

Betty looked at him curiously and back at Alex for confirmation.

"Yes, it is okay, Betty. He knows what's going on," she said, though she wasn't entirely sure why she was trusting him. She didn't know him other than as a passenger on the ship.

"Jane was having an affair with one of the passengers, and the wife found out."

"Where did you get that information?" Alex asked.

"The bartender, of course. They see and hear everything!" Betty replied. "That can't be a coincidence."

"No," Jon replied. "I wouldn't think so."

"By the way, Celia wants us to meet up on the private deck. You know, the one for just our members," Betty said, nodding in Jon's direction. She stood up.

"Sure," Alex agreed. "If you will excuse us, Jon."

Alex stood up. Not waiting for his reply, she and Betty walked away.

On their way out of the yacht club, Alex and Betty grabbed Joey, and the three of them met the others in the private lounge.

Celia immediately asked, "What did the captain say?"

"We didn't see him," Joey replied, standing beside Alex.

"We ran into Kane and met the staff captain, second in charge. He said someone is watching the parents, although I do not know what good that'll do. It is up to us to protect each other and get to the bottom of this."

"Okay, we need a plan," Lucy said.

"Lucy and I will go look for them," Pete volunteered.

"Has anyone seen Jane?" Alex asked the group. "She's either in on it or in trouble."

Betty stood with a tape measure in one hand and a pair of scissors in the other. "I can help," she said.

"Not with those, Betty," Pete said.

Alex arched an eyebrow at Betty's antics and tried to get the discussion back on track. "Okay, we know Arthur came into contact with a harmful plant," Alex said. "Do you remember anything else that might help, Joey?"

"No, Alex. It was all so harmless. I swear."

"I know, Joey." She tried to sound soothing, but she was concerned that they were out of their league. "We can figure this out. The plant was in his parents' cabin. He found it, but why would they keep a dangerous plant in their own room? It doesn't make sense."

"Unless someone else put it there? The person who brought it on board?" Joey suggested.

At that moment, both Betty and Alex said, "Jane." They shared a look of acknowledgement but did not immediately explain.

Pete cleared his throat. "And . . ."

"Sorry, sorry. Betty and I saw Jane carrying a—"

"Plant," Betty interrupted.

"But we didn't make the connection at the time," Alex responded.

"The card. Do you remember, Alex? What did it say?"

"'To my darling wife.'"

"That means Ernesto was the one Jane was having an affair with!" Celia concluded.

"Yes, that makes sense," Pete said. "So Jane brought the plant to their room, thinking of giving it to the wife, trying to harm Birdie? And the son came across it instead?"

"Seems the most likely theory to me," Lucy replied.

"Arthur did say his parents were fighting, and he thought they didn't want him on the trip," Alex added.

"Do you think he wasn't supposed to be on the trip, Alex?" Lucy asked.

"*They* weren't supposed to be on the trip. Birdie *and* Arthur," Alex said, horrified, the pieces of the puzzle starting to come together in her head.

"So if they weren't supposed to be on the trip, it was just going to be what? The husband, Ernesto, and the mistress? Jane?" Pete paused. "But why? If it was supposed to just be Jane and Ernesto, why would she have brought the plant on board?"

"I don't know. Maybe she did expect the wife and son? I think we're still missing something else."

"Maybe we should sleep on it?" Betty suggested.

Celia's phone vibrated. She pulled the phone from her wristlet, unlocked the screen, and read the message. "It is a text from Mimi." She showed Alex.

Gympie Plant, dangerous to the touch.

"Well, I think we're safe from the plant at the moment. I believe Jon saw Birdie throw it overboard," Alex said.

"Who's Jon?" Pete questioned.

"One of the passengers. I met him during the mingles events." At the goo-goo eyes Pete was making, Alex added, "Never mind that. If Birdie knew about Jane, she must've been the one who attacked Jane."

"And you, on the island?" Lucy asked.

"Why would Birdie attack me?" Alex replied.

"Why would any of them attack you, Alex?" Pete responded.

"Alex, the text says the plant is dangerous, not deadly," Joey said, "so how did Arthur die?"

"He died from slipping, falling, and hitting his head. Mimi confirmed it on the island."

"So it was an accident? And he would have lived if he hadn't slipped on a pile of bird kak?" Joey's face squished, and his eyes began to well up with tears. "He was my friend, and we . . ."

Alex could see where his train of thought was headed. "It's not your fault, Joey. I'm not sure exactly, but I know it wasn't the bird pile."

"That still begs the question, why was the plant brought on board?" Betty said.

"And who was the plant supposed to endanger?" Pete added.

"Look, it's late," Alex said. "I don't think there is anything more we can do about this tonight. The staff captain said that security was watching the parents."

"Let's just hope they are watching them better than they were on the island excursion," Celia huffed. "I'm worried about your safety, Alex."

17

SIRENS

THEY EACH SAID THEIR GOOD NIGHTS AND MADE THEIR WAY down the hall to their respective cabins. The door locks chimed one after another as each of her friends entered their rooms.

None of this makes sense. Alex pressed her key card to the lock, opened the door, and entered her suite. *Something went horribly wrong here, and a young man died because of it.*

Alex was about to change when she saw a note on the small writing table.

She reached for it but hesitated. A Windsom logo was embossed at the top of the greeting-card-sized note. Alex grabbed a tissue and used it to carefully pick up the note before reading it.

Meet me on the private deck at 10:30. I will tell you everything!

Alex put the note down on the table and dropped the tissue in the small waste bin under the table. *This has to be from Jane. She's the only one who could access the cabin and the cruise line stationary.*

She went to the sink in the bathroom and rinsed her hands well with soap and water. Alex wasn't sure exactly how the plant was dangerous or if there were more plants on board even. Her mind reeled with questions as she dried her hands on the origami monkey towel hanging from the shower rod. *Is it a trap of some kind? I still don't know which one of them attacked me on the island or why.*

Alex slipped out of her dress and put on a pair of yoga pants and her favorite hoodie. She turned to look at the clock by the bedside table and started. It was already twenty-five past ten! She only had five more minutes. *Did Jane slip into my room when the gang was all in the private lounge? Was it really Jane who left the note? Was it Birdie who attacked me as well as Jane?*

Alex couldn't stop the barrage of questions running through her head as she put on her socks and sneakers. *It could be dangerous. I should tell someone where I'm going.* Alex warred with herself on what she should do. *But I don't want anyone else to get hurt.*

Decision made, she stood up. She was going. Best-case scenario, it was Jane she would confront. Worst-case scenario, what would she do?

I don't know.

The deck was dark when Alex stepped onto the far side of the balcony. She knew right away she was meeting Jane. The shadowy figure was not that of a short robust Italian man nor a slender curvy woman with a wild mane of curly red hair.

Jane spoke from the shadows. "I'm going to help you, Alex. It's the least I can do. I'll come clean . . . for Arthur's sake."

As Alex stepped closer, it was easier to make out the shapes in the shadows. Jane was standing on top of something—a chair or bench, maybe. Another few feet closer and the visibility became clearer. Jane stood on one of the lifeboats, leaning dangerously close to the railing.

"Jane, come down. Come away from the railing so we can talk."

"When I saw the picture of the three of them—a happy little family—I was enraged. It wasn't the plan. This trip was supposed to be for just the two of us." Jane waved her hand wildly. "Go on a cruise. Get the job done. Have fun."

Alex was starting to make sense of the clues. She hadn't realized the meaning of what she'd witnessed at the time. She remembered seeing a picture missing from the message board. She hadn't placed it as a clue at the time, though, when she found the picture of Arthur and his family crumpled up on the floor. In this context, it added up with how Jane had acted toward Birdie that day in quilting class.

"Jane, did Birdie try to kill you?" Alex asked. "When we found you in the hall, I mean. Was it Birdie?"

"I don't know how she found out about Ernesto and me." Jane hesitated for a long minute. "Can you blame his wife for wanting me dead?"

Her voice was growing in agitation. Alex needed to get her down and away from the railing.

"I tried to hurt her by sending her the plant. Instead, I am now responsible for her son's death."

"It wasn't . . ." Alex was about to say it wasn't Jane's fault, but in either scenario, it really was. "Come down from there. We can get some help."

"It was my fault!" Jane shrieked at the top of her lungs. "If I hadn't changed the plan, none of this would have happened."

Why didn't I bring backup with me? I hope all this yelling will arouse someone's suspicion before this becomes a calamity.

Alex crept another few steps in Jane's direction. Thankfully,

Jane didn't move, so Alex asked, "I don't understand, Jane. What plan?"

"What plan? *Our* plan! The plant to—" Jane sighed. "The gympie plant was supposed to make you suffer with pain so bad you would want to kill yourself. It was a brilliant plan. We would never have been suspected."

Make you suffer? Who? "Make who suffer?" Alex asked aloud.

"You, Alex. You were the job. I will tell you everything. I have nothing to lose now, anyway," Jane said, looking over the railing and back at Alex again.

Just when Alex thought Jane was going to step down, two strong masculine hands grabbed Alex from behind. Alex fought to break free. She lunged forward, but her assailant's strength kept her from moving more than an inch.

As she struggled, a dark figure appeared from the opposite side of the deck and pushed Jane. Jane fell backward, her arms flailing, trying to catch onto something before she went over the edge of the railing. Jane's shriek was guttural. Alex screamed in horror. A hand crushed against Alex's mouth, and stifled her cry. Alex waited for a splash but instead came an awful thud.

Oh no, Jane. Alex shuddered then tried to twist around to get a look at their attackers, but there were only two people it could possibly be. *Ernesto and Birdie. They must have followed one of us here.*

"She landed on the deck . . . There's no way she . . ." Ernesto choked out from behind Alex. "You weren't supposed to kill her, Birdie!"

"Shut up, you fool. Don't cry for your mistress," Birdie snapped back at her husband. "We need to take care of this one so we can get out of here. Make it look like an accident." Birdie snarled and advanced on Alex and Ernesto.

STORM AT SEA

ERNESTO'S GRIP LOOSENED EVER SO SLIGHTLY AS HE TRIED to pick Alex up off her feet. In an effort to escape his murderous grip, she lurched forward. The force knocked the two of them to the ground, and Ernesto landed on top of Alex. Alex lost her breath from the force of his weight. Once she had her breath back, she punched him in the kidney as hard as she could. He groaned and rolled off of Alex, and suddenly, she was free of the crippling mass. She jumped to her feet and teetered toward the railing with vertigo from her quick movements. One hand latched on to the cold metal, and she closed her eyes briefly to help the dizziness pass.

Birdie screamed. Pete had a bear-hug grip around Birdie, and she was struggling to break free.

"Quick, Alex. Catch him," he yelled, pointing his chin in Ernesto's direction.

Ernesto was making a run for it. Before Alex had a chance to catch him, he fell face-first onto the floor just inside the lounge. *Betty.*

"Are you all right, Alex?" Betty asked.

"I'm fine. Thank you," Alex looked at the scene to her right.

Pete had something wrapped around Birdie. Alex squinted to see. *It is fabric. A quilt binding?*

"Tie him up, Betty," Pete shouted. "Ow. She bit me!"

"You had better finish this job, or I am going to kill you," Birdie screamed to her husband.

Lucy appeared to Alex's right and hit the emergency button. Sirens blared into the quiet night, and bright white strobe lights flashed around the lounge and out onto the darkness of the deck.

Her Spruce Street family had helped catch the two culprits long before the ship's crack security team arrived.

"This is all your fault," Birdie screamed over the sirens. "What kind of man brings his family along on a hit?"

"Shut up. This is all *your* fault, you wicked woman. This was not supposed to be a *family* vacation," Ernesto boomed back at Birdie as the alarm stopped.

Pete was still struggling to keep hold of Birdie, who was thrashing around like a crazed maniac, and Betty had her scissors to Ernesto's throat.

"Betty!" Pete said and laughed.

Alex shook her head at the foolishness of it, though she had to admit quilt binding did make a nice restraint, and the scissors made a fine weapon after all. She was going to have to remember that for future reference.

"What are you two going on about?" Lucy asked Ernesto.

"Look, lady, I just needed to make her gone." He nodded in Alex's direction. "None of this was supposed to go down this way. After Lilith's screwup—"

"Will you shut up, you big oaf?" Birdie shrieked at her husband.

"I told you not to call me that," he replied. "It was my wife's idea to make this a *family* trip. I just wanted a simple getaway with my—"

Birdie interrupted, spitting the words out. "Your mistress, Jane!"

"And now my son is dead and my . . ." Ernesto said, turning his head to see his wife.

"Don't move. I will cut you," Betty said calmly.

"I should've just killed *you*!" Ernesto glared at his wife until she averted her eyes.

"And now you both are going to jail!" Pete replied.

"It doesn't matter. The partners are going to kill us now that we failed."

Just then, two Windsom security officers rushed in, neither of whom Alex had seen before. One yelled, "Everybody, freeze! No one move!"

"That is what freeze means," Pete said exasperatedly.

"But . . ." Betty said.

Alex glared at her and shushed her with a look.

One by one, they all put their hands up in the air, except Ernesto and Birdie, who were tied up, of course.

"What is going on here?" the taller of the two men asked, speaking up for the first time. He was clearly the other man's superior, despite his younger age.

"Sir," Alex said, "where is Kane? This couple has killed their son. I believe you'll find that they are mafia hit men from New York, and their accomplice . . . Jane . . . is dead." Alex softened and looked over her shoulder.

"I am no hit man. What on earth are you talking about? I only want to kill him," Birdie screeched and spat as the words came out. She struggled trying to break free, trying to attack her husband. "That lying, cheating good-for-nothing. Besides that, we are from Chicago."

The older security man said, "We heard the call of the siren and came in to save the day."

Betty scoffed. "Save the day. I did all your work for you!"

"We," Pete corrected Betty.

"Oh, we know all about these two. Kane's had us watching them for days."

"Clearly not well enough if they were able to come in here and kill one of your co-workers!" Betty said matter-of-factly.

"If you knew these two were bad news, then why did you come rushing in here yelling 'freeze'?" Pete asked.

"Eh, I always wanted to do that!" the guard said.

"Knock it off," his partner scolded and then asked, "Where's the mistress?"

"I told you. She is dead," Alex said.

They all turned to look toward the deck's open doors.

NO LOOSE ENDS HERE

Alex was fuming as she chain-stitched the last row of blocks. She couldn't stop replaying yesterday's meeting with Kane in her head. After the security officers had taken Ernesto and Birdie into custody, Alex had sought out Kane for answers.

She mashed down on the foot pedal a little too aggressively as Kane's words echoed over and over in her mind. "Why don't you and your lady friends just get back to your sewing and stop trying to meddle in the case?" he had asked her, straight-faced.

Just because he saw us breaking into Birdie and Ernesto's room doesn't mean we should be kept out of the loop. Although Alex did feel slightly embarrassed about that.

Though this last leg of the cruise had been uneventful, Alex was in the dark. Birdie and Ernesto were in the brig. Despite Alex's repeated protests, Kane would not allow her access to them or tell her what was happening with the case. She didn't much care for the Windsom security staff as a whole. *They were supposedly 'on task' but had shown up late to the party, only after we had caught the culprits. Storming in to 'save the day.'* Alex scoffed loudly.

She still had unanswered questions, and once they arrived

on land in a few hours, she would lose any chance she had at questioning Birdie and Ernesto.

Alex jumped when she noticed Betty hovering over her. "Geesh, Betty. What's up?"

"Well, I spent the last few nights with Paul." She looked over in Paul's direction and waggled her eyebrows.

TMI, Betty, too much information!

"He is buddies with a couple of the security guys on the overnight shift, you see," Betty continued. "Turns out it was Jane who attacked you in the bathroom. Birdie was blackmailing her. From when Jane tried to kill her and Arthur . . ."

"What a mess," Alex muttered. She stood up and walked to the ironing board to press her finished quilt top. Betty followed.

"The gympie plant was a doozie. I am so glad you did not come in contact with it. Just a couple of hairs from the plant are so painful that it makes people off themselves. One of the guys told Paul he overheard the two of them arguing, Ernesto and Birdie. Turns out Ernesto stole the plant from Birdie's office. You know she is a botanist who studies rare plants in remote parts of the world? Not a stay at home mother as she claimed. Anyway, Ernesto gave the plant to Jane to smuggle onto the ship, but I don't think Jane knew the plant had come from Birdie."

"Okay, and . . ."

"Birdie was drunk. She made a scene in the bar, and everyone was talking about it the next day, and she *is* a serious klepto. They found all sorts of things in her luggage that she had stolen." Betty stared at Alex expectantly but bulldozed on before she could respond. "Which explains why she had your seam ripper in her room."

Alex looked up when Betty hesitated. "And?"

"Well, when she got back to the cabin and then went straight to quilting the next morning . . ." Betty paused. "Well, you know, then we had the mingles event and dinner. By the time Birdie realized the plant was in the room, it was too late. Arthur had already stumbled upon it." Betty cocked her head and raised her eyebrows. "So much for Jane's evil plan to take out the wife. Ernesto brought Jane on the cruise with him, knowing full well *you* were going to be their victim." Betty crossed herself.

"But why would Jane change the plan and try to kill Birdie?"

"Oh, this is where it gets good," Betty said with a mischievous grin. "I was talking to one of the other Windsom staff liaisons for another wealthy couple. She said that Jane went into a rage when she found out that the wife and son were on board the cruise."

"Well, that explains her attitude the first couple quilting sessions. I don't know how you do it, Betty." Alex chuckled.

"It turns out Jane only took the job as our liaison so she could get close to you."

"How did you find that out?"

"From Kane, of course."

"What?"

"Okay, well, I heard it from one of the deckhands who drinks with Kane."

"Betty, really?"

Betty put her hands on her hips and stared at Alex seriously. "Alex, this sleuthing is fun and all, but we keep ending up in these dangerous situations."

"I know, Betty. It's over now," Alex assured her. "Did you finish your quilt top?"

"Yes, of course. I finished it last night. What is taking *you* so long?"

Alex held up her finished quilt top. "Voila."

As she had suspected, Alex was not able to get any more answers or access to Birdie and Ernesto. Alex and Joey stood on the deck and watched the police take the murderous duo off the ship before the passengers were allowed to disembark.

"I can't believe I slept through the sirens, Alex."

"I am glad you were not there, Joey. It was very scary, despite how Betty tells it."

In Betty's version, she had saved the day by apprehending the two criminals with her very own quilting tools, and there was no point in trying to argue with her.

HOME IS WHERE THE DOG IS

"ALASTOR, UNHAND MY DOG," ALEX SAID.

After knocking, she had let herself in. Finding Alastor in his parlor, she had cleared her throat and was horrified to see Alastor appearing to get ready to punt the little dog like a football into his backyard.

"What are you *doing*?" Alex asked, her voice raised but calm.

"This mangy mutt did nothing but bite my ankles the whole time you were gone."

Alex walked over and swiftly removed Kibbles from his grasp.

He pulled his pant leg up to show dozens of tiny puppy bites around his ankle and shin.

"Oh no. I am sorry, Alastor." Thinking better of her sympathy, she added, "But what did you do to this poor little dog? She was peaceful and friendly the entire time Lilith had her, and she's fine with me also."

"This dog doesn't like men!" he insisted. "My brother left early because the dog wouldn't leave him alone either!"

"My goodness." Alex scritched Kibbles on the top of her head. "What did this mwean old mwan do to my wittle sweetheart?" she cooed in baby talk to the dog.

Joey came through the screen door. "Is everything all right, Alex?"

"Watch out," Alastor said, flinching backward, but Kibbles was perfectly calm and allowed Joey to pet her.

"I think she just doesn't like *certain* men, Alastor. See? She's fine with Joey."

Alastor grumbled incoherently. "Okay, you're all home. Now leave me in peace . . . and don't think I am ever going to watch that *murderous mutt* ever again. She should have gone to puppy jail with her owner!"

"Alastor, please," Alex said, and little Kibbles bared her canines. "Look at all these precious wittle teef. You tell that big mean man to be nice to wittle Kibbles."

Joey laughed. "What has gotten into you, Alex?"

Finally home to number 1 on Spruce Street, Alex plopped down in the ugly pig, the most comfortable yet hideous love seat ever. She laughed, thinking fondly of Nona and her favorite love seat. These thoughts reminded her there was a note she still hadn't opened. *Is this the right time to open the letter that said "do not open"?* In all the commotion and chaos, she had forgotten about it.

Alex set Kibbles down next to her and went to her bags in the entryway. She pulled the letter from her bag. *Well, I don't know if this is the right time or not, but you don't just leave a letter saying "don't open" and expect me not to open it.*

Alex,

Somehow, I knew you would open this letter at just the right time. It is the right time now, isn't it?

Oh, I hope you enjoyed your cruise. You deserved a nice, calm, relaxing vacation.

"If she only knew," Alex said and continued reading.

What did you think of Henrietta? She's a gem. You will love her!

How about those kids? Aren't they great!

Well, the last letter covered the logistics of the island. This one's for you, and if you want to share with Jack and Charlotte, I approve.

Now you know who Henrietta is. You have delivered her quilt and used the key to get into my room, which is now your room, and found and read my letters. Now, take my journal and go meet Liam, and don't forget to bring him his quilt. Your next adventure awaits!

~ Nona

What? That's it? Why so secretive? Alex flipped the paper back and forth a couple times to make sure her eyes weren't playing tricks on her. *That's it! What about the skeleton key?*

She still had no resolution on the mysterious key and what it went to, why Nona had left it for her, or why Nona had kept all these things from her and her family.

Alex jumped, startled by the vibration of an incoming text. She pulled the phone out of the back pocket of her favorite jeans. *I really must turn off the vibrate function.*

She looked at the incoming text message. It was from a blocked number.

I am glad you are okay, Alexandra. Liam is the key.

Alex quickly sent a group text to Jack and Charlotte.

There's another letter. Come to #1 for dinner tomorrow night and we can discuss it.

EPILOGUE

ALEX WAS JUST SETTLING BACK INTO LIFE ON SPRUCE Street and preparing for another much-needed quilting retreat. She answered a frantic call from Sue, the owner of Nuts & Bolts Quilt Shop.

"Can we host the quilting retreat at number 1? The store is flooded, and I can't cancel on the quilters with only forty-eight hours' notice!"

"Yes, we can make it work. All has been quiet for months now. Hawk and Mark have been extra vigilant. I see no reason why it wouldn't be an *uneventful* gathering."

She hung up the call with Sue. Her mind was racing with the million things she would need to do in just two days' time to get the house ready for the quilters.

Kibbles stood up on the back of the sofa, barking like mad.

"Kibbles, knock that off! Stop all that barking and gwowling, and put those wittle killer teeffies away," Alex said as she picked the dog up and gave her a squeeze.

Kibbles licked Alex's face in protest.

Alex had grown very fond of the sweet little mutt, and yes,

she had become one of those pet owners that barely said anything coherent when talking to their pet.

Alex opened the curtain, and peered out over Spruce Street. The entire neighborhood was still and quiet.

"See? There's nothing out there. All is calm, Kibbles," she said, but a chill ran up her spine.

Ready to find out what happens next?

Buy Pressing Matters - A Quilting Cozy Mystery
Book 3 in the Quilting Cozy Mysteries Series

Leave a review!

Thank you for reading my book!
I appreciate your feedback and love to hear about how you enjoyed it!

Please leave a positive review letting me know what you thought.

THANK YOU! × × × ×

ABOUT THE AUTHOR

Kathryn Mykel, author of bestselling Sewing Suspicion - A Quilting Cozy Mystery

Inspired by the laugh-out-loud and fanciful aspects of cozies, Kathryn Mykel aims to write lighthearted, humorous cozies surrounding her passion for the craft of quilting.

She was born and raised in a small New England town. She enjoys writing cozy mysteries and short mini mysteries.

For more fun content and new releases, sign up for her newsletter or join her and her thReaders on Facebook at Author Kathryn Mykel or Books For Quilters.

authorkathrynmykelsewingsuspicion.mailerpage.com

Printed in Great Britain
by Amazon

78447286R00097